The Factory

Zak Yates

To Claire

With love

Zak Yates

The Factory

ISBN: 9798649088985

Cover art by Tony Armstrong

The Factory

This book contains themes of an adult nature
and is therefor suitable for mature readers
only.
Strong language, violence and sexual content
throughout.

CHAPTER ONE

Sunday

Peter was fast asleep in his rocking chair outside on his porch dressed in his jeans, denim shirt, cowboy boots and had his favourite white stetson hat on. This was his usual routine in the middle of the afternoon after having a couple of beers and watching the world pass by him. It was a warm, sunny, Sunday afternoon in Driftwood, Texas with not a cloud in the sky. This was the house Peter had grown up in and had moved back to recently. Driftwood was known for being a quiet area, which was just what he had wanted since being laid off from his job at The Factory for having a fight with another co-worker over his marital breakdown. He had been kicked out of his house in Henly by his wife, Brenda, and luckily his mum's house still lay empty from when she had moved out into a nursing home. From what he thought was trying to stick up for himself, it had turned into a full fist fight with Tommy, the workplace sleazebag, who had called him a cheat and shit husband to Brenda. Turned out Tommy and Brenda had actually slept together not long into the marriage and had kept their secret for 6 years until Tommy blurted it out during the fight. Peter was fired straightaway for throwing the first punch, which was 3 months ago now, and Tommy was just told to take a week off.

He hadn't found any work since as there wasn't much around, so now he just wakes up everyday, has a coffee and a cigarette, watches whatever crap is on the television, has his usual cheese sandwich for lunch and then sits on the porch with a couple of beers before taking a nap. He didn't have any friends to talk to, as he had distanced himself from everyone that he used to work with at The Factory. He had been there many years, and was the boss for most of them, but felt like his actions that day had ruined any relationship he'd had with them. Even though he had not found any work yet, he was getting used to his days off, settling into a routine, and enjoying the peace and quiet.

This day would not be a normal day for Peter as he was awoken by someone who he couldn't see as they were standing directly in front of the sun. He must have been in a deep sleep as he never heard the car pull up in front of the house. No words were said, and as Peter lifted his stetson up to see and get a better view of who was there, the gun went off. Peter slumped back in his chair with a bullet hole in his head and blood dripping down his face. This was the end to Peter's routine as he stood over himself looking at what had just happened in shock.

"What the fuck! How can I be...? What's happening?" Peter said, confused as to why he could see himself.

In the moments of confusion as to what was happening to him, he had forgotten to see who'd killed him. He quickly turned around to see who it was but the car was already pulling away, dust flying everywhere, and he couldn't make out the person or car. Thoughts went flying through his head as he sat next to his dead body trying to work out who would have wanted him dead, especially after not seeing anyone, or hearing from anyone for 3 months, and only ever calling the nursing home to check on his mum who had dementia. Even she didn't know who he was anymore but it made him feel better that he called. He sat next to his body and tried to touch the shoulder of his dead self but quickly pulled away as the strange feeling of going through another body scared him.

"I can walk, sit down on things but can't touch other beings. This is fucking weird," he muttered to himself as he sat there waiting for someone to find him, call the police or do anything. But no one came and no one called as no one ever did. As he sat there, he knew he would have to find his killer himself, but where to start?

"Jonny may know."

Within seconds of thinking about seeing Jonny, Peter arrived in Woodcreek at the Hideaway Tavern to find Jonny sitting alone on a bar stool with a large whiskey in front of him. He wasn't with anyone or talking with anyone, just sitting there staring into his glass. Wearing his usual combination of blue jeans, black t-shirt, black leather jacket and brown cowboy boots, Peter could spot him from a mile off. Now in his early 40s, Jonny hadn't altered from when Peter had met him 10 years ago at the Factory; slightly stocky build, always had a buzzed hair cut and facial stubble, and when not at work he had these exact same clothes on. Very predictable. The bar was pretty empty with only a couple of young lads playing darts, and two others slow dancing next to the jukebox, which had Dolly Parton's version of 'I Will Always Love You' playing. You could tell what the outcome of that dance would be as the man, who looked like he'd had plenty to drink already, kept grabbing the woman's arse every moment he could, and as she would lift his hand back up, he would slide it straight back down. The bar was dimly lit as it was almost closing time, which was a bit earlier on a Sunday night compared to the rest of the week, but the smell of cigarette smoke was still in the air as this was one of the few places that still let people smoke indoors and was popular with the old men of Woodcreek, who liked a beer and cigar without having to move off their bar stools.

The bartender was drying the glasses that had just been washed and walked past Jonny.

"Is everything alright?" he asked.

Jonny didn't reply, he just sat in silence still watching the ice melt, so the bartender just walked away and carried on putting the glasses away, tidying up ready to close. Peter took a seat next to him.

"Hey man, I need your help," Peter said, trying to get Jonny's attention.

Jonny didn't flinch from his position; he just kept staring at his glass.

"Listen, I've been shot and need to find out who did it," Peter continued a little louder in case the sound of Dolly's voice was drowning him out.

Another pause, and still no movement. Peter tried waving and clicking his fingers at both Jonny and the bartender. Then it dawned on Peter that not only could no one see him, they also couldn't hear him.

"Fucking brilliant! All these questions and no fucking answers. This is gonna be harder than I thought," he said, swivelling himself round, folding his arms on the bar feeling defeated.

A few minutes went by when, as the bell

rang for last call, Jonny went to lift his glass up. The bartender noticed that the knuckles on Jonny's right hand were bruised and cut, but before he could say anything, Jonny had clocked his face and quickly removed his right hand from the glass and swapped to his left, picking the glass up and knocking back the whiskey.

"What have you done to your hand?" Peter asked. Then the realisation hit again. "Oh shit, yeah, this is gonna take some getting used to."

The glass slammed down on the bar and the bar stool scraped the floor as Jonny stood up. He pulled out a $20 bill, put it by his glass and headed for the door, not wanting or waiting for the change. That was clearly enough for Jonny. Maybe it was the fact that the couple dancing had put the same song on again and he couldn't cope with a double dose of Dolly, or that he could only handle one drink these days. Peter got up and followed him out.

Jonny walked outside, stood by the door and pulled his smokes out of the inside pocket of his jacket. He lit a cigarette, took a few drags, and started to walk down the steps outside the bar, slowly taking his time. It was quite a warm night, as it was most nights in the middle of June, and the moon was full, shining its light all over, casting shadows of the trees that lined the street opposite the tavern. A few hundred yards to the right, standing under a street lamp, Jonny noticed there was a group of four prostitutes standing together waiting for passers by.

"Can't be much trade around here, it's too quiet," Peter commented, also seeing them standing there.

Jonny starting walking towards them. As he got closer, he finished his cigarette and threw it to the ground, reached in his other inside pocket and pulled out a roll of 20s.

"Who wants this?" Jonny asked, waving it around like food to a pet.

"You dirty bastard," Peter remarked, shaking his head.

Within seconds of the girls seeing the money, he could have his pick as they flocked like vultures to a feed, not giving a shit and just wanting a quick shag for the night. Jonny picked the tall, skinny, blonde girl who was wearing a very small black mini-skirt that only just covered her arse, and a white crop-top with no bra as he could see her perked breast underneath.

"So sugar, where are you gonna take me?" she whispered in his ear, stroking his crotch to get him hard.

"She doesn't waste any time," Peter said, watching her go in for the kill.

"I've got a room ready, don't you worry," he replied as she linked his arm and started walking towards the car park of the tavern where he had left his car. There was only one light shining down on a few cars that were parked up, which must have been left there from the night before as there weren't many people in tonight. Peter knew which car was Jonny's and tried his thinking trick again, which worked, and he appeared inside the car, watching the two approach. The prostitute was stroking Jonny's back and arse whilst walking and came across some more round lumps which were in his back pockets, the same shape as what was just waved in front of her face just moments ago. She went in for a kiss to distract Jonny, but nothing got past him. He let her put her hand in and take the cash thinking she was in, but they had just reached the car and within a split second, Jonny grabbed the prostitute's head, pulled her hair tightly, and slammed her face into the side of the car.

"Fucking thieving bitch," he whispered into her ear as he pulled her head back.

"Holy shit," shouted Peter as he jumped back in his seat, shocked by the sound of the girl's head hitting the car.

He slammed her head against the car for a second time; sex was now the last thing on Jonny's mind. The sound of the girl's head hitting the car the second time had pulled the attention of the other prostitutes, who were still standing under the street lamp waiting for their chance.

"What the fuck! Get off her!" screamed one of the girls as they started running to help.

"Oi, dickhead! Get your fucking hands off her," shouted another girl.

They couldn't reach the car in time as Jonny had already opened the trunk, thrown the blonde in, and was speeding out of the car park. Peter turned to see the girls running into the bar to no doubt call the police.

Racing out of Woodcreek at high speed, Peter, still in shock, turned and looked at

Jonny. "Who the fuck are you?" he questioned whilst they drove away in the moonlight.

Although Peter knew Jonny very well from working together at The Factory for many years, before Jonny left - well, was sacked due to his drinking problem and always being late - he was his first stop to try and find out who had shot him, yet after what he had just witnessed, Peter was sitting there wondering if Jonny could have killed him himself. They were travelling so fast that Peter could not tell which direction they were going, and then suddenly the car skidded to a stop. Jonny quickly got out of the car and slammed the door, reaching for his cigarettes.

"Fuck! Fuck! Fuck!" said Jonny whilst pacing up and down, kicking stones, clearly angry and upset, shaking his head.

"Just what have you done?" Peter said, looking in shock at Jonny as he also got out of the car.

"What made you do this?" Peter asked again, waiting for a reply.

The reply that would never come as he couldn't hear him.

'Has he done this kind of thing before?'

13

was the thought running through Peter's mind as he watched Jonny pace around, clearly wondering what to do next. Then, like a light bulb moment, Jonny went to the trunk and opened it to get the girl out. As the trunk opened the girl swung for Jonny with a wrench she had found.

"You bastard!" she yelled, yet blood was still dripping down her face so her aim was off and she missed him.

Jonny slammed the trunk down, trapping the girl's arm on the outside by her elbow.

"Holy fuck!" shouted Peter, who couldn't believe what he was watching.

The girl screamed in agony as Jonny held her hand where it was and slammed the trunk down again, this time snapping the girl's forearm completely off from the elbow. If the sound of the crack wasn't enough, the amount of blood that splattered everywhere was making Peter feel sick to his stomach and he had to turn away. There was no coming back from this as Peter had just seen Jonny go from just wanting sex to chopping the arm off a woman.

"What the fuck is wrong with you?" Peter asked Jonny, shaking his head in disgust and shame.

Jonny wasn't finished though, and still with rage on his face and a look Peter had never seen before on him, he opened the trunk and dragged the girl out of the car, throwing her to the floor. She tried to stand up but he kicked her down again making her body roll, leaving her on her back. She grabbed hold of her arm that was still gushing with blood and was screaming as loud as she could, but there was no one around for miles to hear her.

"Shut the fuck up, you stupid whore," he yelled to her as he started kicking her all over.

"Jesus Christ man, stop!" cried Peter, but Jonny was angry and kept kicking and kicking until her body wasn't moving. "Is she dead?" Peter asked, moving closer and seeing her body lying there, lifeless.

Thinking that was it, Peter then saw Jonny reaching back into his trunk and pulling out a screwdriver. Rolling the girl's body on her back, Jonny stabbed her straight through the heart as he wanted to be sure she was dead.

"Holy fuck, you evil psycho," Peter said while he could do nothing but watch Jonny butcher this poor girl.

There was blood everywhere, dripping

from Jonny's car and all over the road. This was a mess that could not be left. Standing back, Jonny realised just what he had done.

"Shit!" Jonny screamed at the top of his voice.

Looking around, he knew it couldn't be left like this, so he grabbed the girl's butchered body and threw it back in the trunk of his car. He took out his petrol can and started pouring whatever petrol was in it all over the car and inside the trunk, making sure some covered the blood on the road. He stood back, lit a cigarette, took two drags and threw it at the car. The car ignited into a full blaze within seconds and Jonny just turned and walked away. Peter stopped for a second to try and take in what had just happened, then turned and looked over his shoulder to see Jonny just walking away in the moonlight without a care in the world.

Peter waited a little longer to see if he would meet the ghost of the dead girl, but no one showed up, which puzzled him. 'Was it because she already knew her killer?' he pondered, 'and that's why she's not appeared?' It was the only explanation he could come up with as he turned to catch up with Jonny to see what he was up to.

CHAPTER TWO

Monday

Peter followed Jonny on foot for hours, walking west as the sun was rising behind them, casting a shadow of Jonny in front of them. They saw a sign for Blanco which was 4 miles away and that was where Jonny lived. Peter noticed that Jonny looked pale and weak as he had not eaten anything since the day before but, still in shock at what he had just witnessed, was now thinking that it could have been Jonny that had killed him, and if so, why?

"So come on, spit it out, why did you kill me?" Peter started. "What did I do to deserve this?" he carried on.

Another hour passed and not one of Peter's questions was answered. They finally reached Blanco, and just as they were coming to the top of Jonny's road, his phone rang.

"Hey, what's up?" Jonny answered, knowing who it was and acting like nothing had happened.

Peter stood and listened to the whole conversation and then there it was, the proof he'd been looking for to find out if Jonny had killed him.

"Brenda, I was with you all day yesterday and then I went for a drink on my way home."

"And has just murdered someone," sneaked in Peter, mid-conversation.

"I had to get a taxi back as I was over the limit, can you make your own way to work?" Jonny questioned. "I'll pop by just before you finish."

Peter knew there and then that it couldn't have been Jonny that shot him, as he was shot in the middle of the afternoon and he'd just said he was with…

"Hang on a minute, is this my Brenda you're talking to?" asked Peter, who looked startled.

Was this his wife he was talking to, and was she sleeping with Jonny too, as well as Tommy? Brenda was hiding more than he knew, but was now in real danger, as Jonny had just dismembered a girl and set her on fire, and he was potentially going to see her later.

"Don't you fucking touch her," Peter said.

He knew he had to see what Brenda was up to first, and find out if she had anything to do with his death.

With a thought, Peter appeared on the street standing outside Billy's Burger Barn where he and Brenda had first met. It was 8:25am as he knew that she showed up at the same time every morning like clockwork, as her shift started at 8:30. It was a warm, sunny Monday morning with a slight breeze blowing from the east. Brenda had been working at Billy's for many years and it was a favourite spot for The Factory workers at lunchtime especially as the food was nice and quick and it was only a short drive west from The Factory on the E Highway 290 in Dripping Springs. Whilst standing waiting for her, the memories of the first time they met came flooding back. He remembered being sat in his usual booth in the corner with co-workers Tommy, Jonny and Paul so they could see everything and everyone, when Brenda had come over to take their order. The smile and wink she had given him when she'd slipped her phone number to him just before they left to go back to work he could never forget. With Peter knowing what he knew now, he was wondering just how many times she gave her phone number out, and had it even stopped while they were married, especially after he'd found out about Tommy. A taxi pulled up and out got Brenda in her pink and white Billy's Burger Barn uniform, her hair all permed and so much makeup on that you wouldn't recognise the woman underneath. She had a slender figure, but what drew most guys' attention was her great set of tits that she used to love to show off, pushing them together in her tight bra so they virtually popped out of her uniform. She headed inside and Peter followed, taking a seat in the corner where they first met, watching her start work.

"Morning, Billy," she shouted through to the kitchen from behind the counter.

"Morning, Brenda love," Billy replied, cooking away.

There were only a couple of people in, ready for their breakfast before they started work.

"Hey, Jay," Brenda said as Janine, the other waitress who had already been in since 6am on the early shift, passed by with a jug of coffee in the hand.

"Hey girl, looking good," she replied as she headed towards the booth furthest away from Peter.

The smell of fried bacon and sausages oozed through the barn, which would make anyone hungry when they walked in. Peter watched on as she took orders and smiled at everyone, a smile he really missed, especially in the morning, when he used to wake her up with a fresh cup of coffee before driving her to work. Not long into her shift, the door opened and in walked Tommy, looking as dashing as ever, like most sleazebags do, with his tight black pants, white shirt opened up at the top, sleeves rolled up to show off his muscles, and long dark brown hair combed back off his face. He looked directly at Brenda, nodded and smiled and sat right opposite Peter. Still pissed off with Tommy, Peter stood up.

"You bastard!" Peter yelled as he tried to punch Tommy in the face and realised, as his fist went right through Tommy's face, it was no use as it couldn't hurt him, so he sat back down in frustration and waited for Brenda to come over. While Tommy was reading the menu, Brenda sneaked up and sat directly across from him and pulled the menu down.

"Hey, gorgeous," she said whilst putting her foot between Tommy's legs to tease him.

"Woah, not in public, what if someone sees?" he replied whilst pulling himself back in his seat.

"I can see everything, thank you, you little shitbag," Peter blurted out, staring at Tommy.

Peter sat and watched the two flirt, eyes gazing into each others with grins like naughty school children.

"Can I get a Billy's Delight?" Tommy asked.

"I thought you preferred my delights," Brenda quickly responded, pushing her tits closer to Tommy across the table.

"That was last week; this week it's Billy's turn," Tommy smirkingly commented back.

"You cheeky bugger," she replied, throwing her notepad at him.

Peter, watching all of this flirting, realised that it wasn't just the one time they'd slept together, this had been going on all the way through their marriage, and yet it was Tommy who had called Peter a cheat, and that was what had gotten him fired from The Factory.

"You cheating bastards, the pair of you," Peter noted whilst looking at them more than once.

Even though Brenda had kicked Peter out soon after he got fired, they were technically still married as they had not filed for divorce yet, so it could have been Tommy who shot Peter to get him out of the way, so he could have Brenda all to himself.

"You're not the only one, you do know that, don't you?" Peter said to Tommy as Brenda collected her notepad and left the table, stroking her fingers through his hair like she used to with Peter. Little did Tommy know that Brenda was also seeing Jonny too, but Jonny was with Brenda yesterday, so where was Tommy?

"Coffee hun?" asked Janine as she made her way over towards Tommy.

"Sweet and creamy, just like you," he said as he looked her up and down.

As she was pouring, he slid his hand up her uniform skirt and squeezed her arse.

"Same again sometime?" he asked, letting

go of her cheek and stroking her leg on the way down.

"Maybe," she said as she walked away.

"You really are a piece of work, you know that?" Peter remarked at Tommy's actions.

Brenda arrived back over with Tommy's food; the Billy's Delight, which was just poached eggs on a muffin with Billy's secret sauce and placed it in front of him.

"Have this delight now and you can have my delights later," she whispered in his ear.

"Oh shut up, you slag," remarked Peter, who got up from the table. "I don't think I can take much more of this, you're making me sick," he said as he walked to the counter and sat on a stool where he could still see Tommy but not have to deal with the childish flirtations going on between them. Tommy finished his breakfast and walked towards Brenda who was now standing by the till.

"There you go, sweetheart," he said whilst passing her a $10 bill. "Keep the change," he added whilst winking and backing away.

"Call me," Brenda replied as she smiled and waved, watching him leave.

As Tommy turned to leave he clocked Janine near the door. "Later," he mouthed, to which she just smiled back.

Peter got up from his stool and headed towards the door. Tommy was not going out of Peter's sight until he knew if he was the one or not.

After feeling sickened at watching Tommy and Brenda flirt so much over breakfast, it was time for Peter to follow Tommy and see just who he was. Peter knew Brenda was safe for now as she didn't finish her shift until 6:30pm, and he would be back in time to make sure she got home okay and that Jonny wouldn't harm her. Even though he knew he couldn't physically stop anything, he still wanted to try and protect her; she was still his wife, a cheating whore, but still his wife. Peter appeared in Tommy's car and went with him to work, back to The Factory that Peter hadn't stepped foot in for the 3 months since he was fired.

Just off the E Highway 290 was a single road that lead to a car park. This was private land and had 'No Entry' signs dotted all the way down the path. Purpose built at the end of the road was a large four-storey building guarded by a steel fence with barbed-wire circling the top. To enter, there was a security checkpoint at the main gate where every employee had to show their ID badge to get through.

Known as The Factory, this was a highly secure building that stored government secrets. Not many that worked at The Factory knew what these secrets were, except for just the senior managers, which George and Derek were. George had been training under Peter, before Peter was fired for the fight, and had got promoted to manager instantly by Derek, the senior manager. Derek was a bit of a dick most of the time as he always thought he was better than everyone else, just because he had more access than most to classified information. His name got brought up on many occasions when people wanted to rant - it was just too easy. He liked to be called DD because his name was Derek Dilingham but everyone just knew it as Dickhead Derek.

The ground floor consisted of toilets, a locker room for personal belongings, a lounge with a large widescreen TV, and down the corridor, the canteen which not many people ate at, especially when Billy's was just down the road and was nicer. The first floor was where the majority of the staff worked. Work stations were dotted around the entire floor, all with desktop computers. No laptops were allowed so that nothing could leave the facility. The second floor had the most impressive amount of hard drives anyone had seen. Rows and rows of machines all lined up, collecting data that the staff had found and then finally there was third floor, the floor the staff enjoyed.

Known as the Recreation Room, half of the floor had games, video games, plus various different activities to do, whilst the other half of the floor had relaxation activities with soundproof pods for meditation and yoga mats ready to use. The working day was quite long, with shifts being 12 hours long from 9am-9pm, with a small number of workers that did nights. Management had realised they got more out of the staff when they were relaxed and not stressed, so had had this floor converted, giving staff a 45-minute break in the morning and another 45 minutes in the afternoon, plus an hour for lunch. This made staring at a computer screen for hours more bearable.

Walking in felt really strange as he had not seen anyone from here for what felt like such a long time. Peter followed Tommy to the locker room where he was hanging up his jacket, and noticed that in Tommy's locker was a picture of him and Brenda by a lake.

"No she didn't," Peter muttered.

This was the same spot she had taken Peter to not long after they'd got married. It must have been a spot she took all her male friends to. Paul, Sheila, Terry and George all walked in to put their coats away ready to start a new week at work.

"Hey Tommy, how are you?" asked Sheila. "Was it your usual Monday morning breakfast today?"

"Yes of course, at Billy's" replied Tommy.

"Was Brenda there today?" asked George.

Tommy went straight over to Paul and pulled him aside.

"Yes she was, and she got me hard while I was eating my poached eggs," whispered Tommy

"I heard that! I'm gonna be sick," shouted Sheila from the other side of the room.

"Leave the poor lad alone," added George.

He was like that, Tommy, just pushed his sex life in everyone's faces, yet how no one found out about those two whilst Peter worked there he didn't quite get. Paul just shook his head as he was quite a shy guy and didn't really say much; most just felt sorry for him and always invited him out with them to include him. Peter went over to peer in Paul's locker while he was getting ready and noticed that in his locker, Paul also had a picture of him and Brenda at the same lake.

"What the fuck is going on?! Not you too," Peter said with a surprised look on his face.

Peter was now wondering if Paul was shagging his wife too, and if these two guys were that clueless that they both had the same picture in their lockers and never noticed.

"I'm coming back for you," Peter said in Paul's face as he knew he couldn't follow two people at once, and it was Tommy he had his eyes on.

As Peter followed Tommy out of the locker room towards the staircase he noticed Tommy winking at all the girls who worked there and when Shirly passed by, holding the accounts that she had brought in with her, he slapped her on the arse.

"Piss off, you prick," she replied.

He then made the phone sign with his

right hand. "Call me," whispered from his lips.

"Screw you!" And with a flash of the V signs she walked away.

It looked to Peter that Tommy was a sleazebag and a slag, and was sleeping with many of his co-workers. He was one of those guys who didn't give a crap about what people thought about him as he loved himself way too much and probably had every sexually transmitted disease going. As they reached Tommy's work-station, Peter stood right opposite him and stared him right in the face, trying to figure out a reason why it could be Tommy that had turned up at his house and shot him without saying a word.

"Were you jealous of me?" Peter asked, which was doubtful, seeing how many people he was probably shagging. He had already had his wife more times than he'd like to think about, but was there something else? Nothing was coming to mind and the longer Peter stared, the more he just wanted to smack Tommy right between the eyes. Peter walked around the floor he used to work on looking at all of his other co-workers, wondering if any of them could have killed him, but he wasn't friends with most of them so they would have no reason to.

A text came through to Tommy's phone, which was so loud that everyone could hear it; an insecurity thing to say to everyone that he was popular, yet Peter knew he hardly had any mates from the amount of drunken phone calls he used to get at the weekend, pretending he was out at clubs having a piss up, yet you could hear his mum watching reruns of Dallas on TV in the background. No one was meant to know that his mum lived with him, but Peter had dropped him off a couple of times and had noticed his mum in the kitchen window waiting for him to come in. This couldn't be the reason he shot Peter, surely? Many still live with their parents but it did cross Peter's mind, until he read the text which was from a number, not a name, and all it said was 'Is it done', to which Tommy text back 'Yes!'.

Peter was now thinking, was it Tommy? Was he made to do it? And who does that phone number belong to? The phone went straight back in his pocket and he stood up quickly, looking slightly nervous and worried. Peter followed as Tommy quickly made his way to the bathroom, straight to the nearest sink and splashed cold water in his face. He looked up with water dripping down his face, looking at himself in the mirror.

"FUCK!" he shouted very loudly.

Quickly drying his face with the paper towels that were on the side, Tommy composed himself and left the bathroom, heading straight to Derek's office. He knocked and entered without waiting for a response.

"Hey, DD, I've got a family emergency and need to leave right away."

"Okay no worries, call me later and let me know when you'll be back in," Derek responded.

"Will do, cheers," said Tommy as he closed the door behind him.

Without saying a word to anyone, despite everyone looking at him as they had heard him shouting, he left the floor and headed to the locker room to collect his things. Grabbing his coat, he slammed his locker shut and headed for the front door, car keys at the ready. Jumping in the passenger seat right next to him, Peter was now intrigued as to what he was up to and who it would lead to.

The radio went on full blast as Tommy reversed out of the factory car park and sped down the side street towards the main highway. He had his foot down, clearly in a hurry to get somewhere. He was overtaking everyone that was in his way, only just missing the red lights in front of them.

"Fucking hell man you're gonna get me killed," cried Peter. "Oh wait, yeah, never mind," he added, answering himself.

Peter was looking at Tommy, and out of the window, wondering where they were headed in such a rush. What did that text mean? Was his killer about to be revealed to him? They passed Sunset Valley, staying on the 290 heading east when Peter realised Tommy must be heading home, which was in Travis Heights. Most of The Factory workers lived in Travis Heights as the company had a deal with a housing firm that they rented houses or flats to workers for cheap.

The car pulled up outside Tommy's house and he got out and rushed to the door, scrambling for the front door key. Throwing the front door open, and leaving it wide open, he went to his bedroom and reached around under his bed, pulling out a large black suitcase. Opening all different drawers around the room, Tommy started throwing in random clothes and belongings. Peter pulled up a chair and sat watching whilst the panic in the room was intense. Everything was being flown everywhere, with only some things actually making the suitcase. His phone kept ringing but Tommy just looked at the screen and threw it on the bed every time, obviously not wanting to talk to anyone.

"Where are you running off to, you lying sack of shit?" Peter hurled over at Tommy.

He was clearly spooked by that text he got at The Factory and was doing a runner. He dragged the suitcase down the hall and went into his mum's room, heading straight for the top cupboard of her built-in wardrobes, knowing that his mum kept some savings up there. Grabbing as much as he could, he stashed the money in his front pocket, the suitcase was in hand and the front door slammed behind him. On his way to the car he clicked a button on his key ring to open the trunk and he flung his suitcase in.

A car came speeding round the corner. It

was a black 4x4 with blacked out windows and as it got closer it seemed to slow down. Tommy turned around quickly, shutting the trunk, when the passenger window of the car opened and a gun came pointing out. Tommy's face dropped as knew who it was when four rounds were shot directly into Tommy's chest and heart.

"Holy fuck! What is going on?" Peter yelled as he also ducked.

The window went back up and the car carried on as Tommy's body started to slump down by the rear tyre. Peter didn't get a chance to see who it was as he was too worried about Tommy gasping for breath. Tommy was dying right in front of him.

"What have you been up to that's got you killed in the middle of the day?" Peter asked, staring directly into Tommy's eyes.

How was Peter now going to know if Tommy shot him or not, with Tommy lying there on the ground and another car driving off in the distance? All he wanted to know was who shot him and why.

Returning back to Driftwood, Peter stood by the steps of his house and looked at where he was shot, yet there was nothing there. No body and no blood. The scene of his murder had been wiped clean like it had never happened. He sat in the chair that had left a bullet hole in his head and rocked back and forth, hoping to figure out some answers as to who could have wanted him dead, and now, who had moved his body. Someone really didn't want anyone to know he was missing, and Tommy was now out of the picture, but what he was up to was puzzling Peter. Did Brenda have anything to do with this, was the quiet, shy Paul a cold-hearted killer, or was he missing something else? Then it dawned on him; all this time looking for his killer he had forgotten the one person he had kept up with since losing his job: his mum in the nursing home. He couldn't call her, but he could actually go and see her now, and with a thought, he was there.

Sat on a floral design, high back chair, wearing a long-pleated pale blue skirt and a white blouse with a pale blue cardigan covering her shoulders was Peter's mum, Pauline. She had been in the nursing home for a little over two years now after being diagnosed with dementia at the age of 83, and had been struggling to live at home by herself. Peter's dad, Herbert, or as everyone else used to call him, Herbie, had died when Peter was 12 years old in a car crash on his way home from the shops, leaving Pauline to look after Peter on her own. She never did find anyone else after Herbie died as all her love went to Peter instead. Peter watched his mum slowly lose her memory, and over the years she had started to forget more and more each time he went to visit. As he was still working full time when she was diagnosed, the only option was to move her into a home to get the help she needed. The Hawthorne Nursing Home in Wimberley, which specialised in caring for anyone with all forms of dementia, was the closest Peter could find in the area. It was quite a large home which housed around 60 residents over 3 floors. Pauline was on the ground floor as she used to like sitting out in the garden watching the birds fly by. Today she was sitting inside, in the communal lounge looking out of the window, watching the world pass by but with hardly any expression on her face, just the occasional blink and lick of her lips. Sat across from her, Peter felt so guilty for not being there for his mum and for not being able to do anything for her now. He couldn't even let her know he was dead; no one could as no one knew. Only his murderer, who he couldn't find.

"Hi mum, I'm here for you now. I've missed you," he said, leaning in closer to her.

A carer came over, a pretty girl with long dark hair, and popped a drink of water down on the table next to where Pauline was sitting. The dark purple top she had on as part of her uniform really suited her, thought Peter as he tried to search for her name, but her hair was covering her name tag and he couldn't get a good view.

"There you go, Pauline, I'll be back round soon with some cookies."

She left to distribute the rest of the drinks out to the other eleven people in the lounge who were also just sitting there. Some were watching television, one man shouting for Betty every 20 seconds - Peter could only presume that is or was his wife's name - and another lady who was wheeling herself around the lounge in her wheelchair, trying to steal everyone's cookies. Peter watched this lady come past his mum and bump into her chair.

"You're always in the way you. Move that damn chair!" this lady yelled at Pauline.

After hitting the chair several times she wheeled herself off, all the time Pauline keeping her same expression, and she didn't move her head from the same position looking out of the window.

Peter sat across from his mum for almost 30 minutes, talking to her about what had happened to him and how he was on a mission to find out who had killed him when the same young carer who had brought the water over earlier came back to see why the water had not been touched.

"Pauline. Pauline. Pauline," called the carer as she tapped her shoulder.

"Nurse, can you come here a moment please?" she said as she looked over the other side of the room.

Peter realised something was wrong. The expression on his mother's face had not changed but the blinking had stopped. The nurse came over, she was a large lady with the biggest afro hairstyle Peter had ever seen. Checking her vital signs in front of him, Peter sat back to take in that his mum had passed away right there in front of him, and all the time he had been talking, he hadn't noticed. The nurse looked at the carer and shook her head.

"Can you wheel Pauline back to her room please and get her changed," the nurse said quietly to the carer.

"Of course," replied the carer.

The chair Pauline was sat on had wheels so that it was easily movable to and from rooms when needed, so the carer pushed the chair out of the living room and down the end of the corridor to room number 14. None of the other residents had noticed as Pauline had never really been a talker ever since she'd moved in, so they had just carried on watching the television as she passed them. Her room was virtually empty with just a bed, single wardrobe, small chest of drawers and two paintings of rivers running through forests hanging on different walls. No pictures of the family or any personal belongings were out as Pauline had packed them in her suitcase before breakfast, as she always thought she was leaving that day and packed a case in the morning. The staff used to have to go in during tea time and unpack it for her so she could follow the same routine the next day.

The carer that had wheeled Pauline back to her room was now joined by another, a young lad, who helped hoist Pauline's body onto her bed. They laid her body out, washed her down and changed her clothes, which Peter thought made her look ever so peaceful. As the carers were finishing off, tucking the blanket in, the nurse appeared, holding a single white rose, and walked over to Pauline and placed it in her hands.

"Goodnight sweetheart, rest in peace," the nurse said as she placed her hands on Pauline's. Peter stood by the bed watching all of this happen and was so thankful to the staff for everything they had done.

"Goodnight mum, I love you," Peter whispered in his mother's ear, leaning over the side of the bed.

He attempted to kiss her on the forehead which didn't work and stood back up. Peter was now alone with his mother as everyone had left, closing the door behind them. He could hear the nurse down the corridor, as the room they were in was not far from the nurse's station, talking to the doctor and asking for someone to pass her Pauline's file and get the next of kin's number. Peter walked to the nurse's station.

"I'm already here," he said as he placed both hands on the worktop.

The nurse finished her call to the doctor and called Peter's home phone and, when no one answered, she tried his mobile. The phone kept ringing and ringing and there was still no answer.

"No one's going to pick up, love, I'm here, dead," Peter uttered as he looked directly at the nurse.

She tried both numbers again to no avail and had to stop as the undertakers needed to be informed. Peter went back to be with his mother as there was no point standing by the station talking to himself. He knew that her funeral would be okay as she had already paid for a plan many years beforehand, so that Peter would never have to worry about it. Suddenly, Pauline's door flung open and Peter's sister, April, rushed in.

"Oh, mum, look at you," she said, rushing to the side of the bed. "You look beautiful." She placed a hand on her mum's and kissed her forehead.

Peter hadn't seen April in nearly 20 years as she had fallen out with the whole family, run off with a drug dealer, and got herself pregnant. Peter was stunned as to why she was here and how she knew where his mum was, as he had not told her. The young female carer that Peter had seen earlier followed April in.

"You made it, then," the carer said whilst walking to the opposite side of the bed to stand next to Peter.

"Well, not in time to say goodbye, but I'm here now," snapped April.

"It was very sudden as there was no change since you last saw her."

"'Last saw her'," Peter jumped in. "When were you here last?" he asked April.

"I know, she didn't recognise me then either," April replied whilst looking at her mum's face.

"Has Peter been in yet?" she asked the carer.

"We can't seem to get hold of him," the carer replied, shrugging her shoulders.

"Don't worry, I'll see him later and tell him."

Peter paused and looked directly at April. "Just what are you up to?"

April had never been to Peter's house and didn't have his phone number, or so he thought.

"Tomorrow, 7:30pm, Waywood Inn. Be there," said April.

"I had to book the night off," replied the

carer as she started to walk towards the door.

"Is that my problem?" April asked. "There's one last job you have to do before it's over."

"Anything for this to be over," replied the carer as she walked towards the door, closing it without looking back.

Standing there listening to April and the carer talk, he realised that's how April knew where their mum was living: this carer had given her the information. She must have also given Peter's details to her too, which was how April knew where he lived. As the carer left and closed the door, Peter wondered if she had also given his details to his killer too. There was something going on with April and that carer that he couldn't quite put his finger on, but he would be there tomorrow at 7:30pm when they meet up to find out.

The undertakers arrived and April was asked to leave the room whilst they did their job. Peter stood outside the door waiting to see his mum off, but April had walked off and was waiting outside the elevator, putting on her leather jacket. The lipstick came out of her small handbag and she was piling it on like she was going on her very first date. Peter turned towards his mum's room as the door had just been opened, and when he turned back to see if April was waiting, she had already gone. He knew she was a heartless bitch but this was something else. She was up to no good and after something. He stood there and watched his mum pass by him in a body bag on a silver trolley, wishing now that he had left beforehand as when they got to the elevator, they tilted the body upright and rolled her in, like she was some sort of parcel out for delivery. It wasn't the last memory he really wanted of his mum as the elevator doors closed. Before he left, he wanted to know what this carer's name was. He tracked her down in the kitchen and noticed she wasn't making tea or coffee but actually stealing some medication.

"So that's what you're up to," remarked Peter whilst peering over her shoulder.

She was taking pills out of various residents' pots and was wrapping them up in tissue paper, putting them in her pocket. All Peter could do was look at her name tag, which said Lisa. Was this her real name or not, and was she supplying drugs to his sister?

CHAPTER THREE

Tuesday

Paul, Sheila, Terry and George were all standing in The Factory's smoking shelter, it was 11:30am and they were coming to the end of their Tuesday morning 45-minute break. Shielding from the rain that had suddenly just come down, they huddled together in the back corner of the shelter so they didn't get wet, each lighting their cigarettes as Paul passed around his lighter. Peter had appeared to see if any of them knew anything or had heard about Tommy after yesterday. He had worked with these guys for ages and really wanted their help. They were the only smokers left in The Factory and if anyone knew how to gossip, it was them.

Paul and Terry had been there the longest,

even though they were the youngest and in their late 20s. Sheila was in her mid-40s with George being the latest recruit; he was the eldest, in his early 50s. All of them were smartly dressed as that was now company policy. Even though they were stuck behind a desk all day, for some reason the company had put a dress code in place. They had all left their coats inside though, as when they had come out, it was still sunny.

"This fucking rain does my head in," George said out of the blue.

"It's good for my garden," replied Sheila.

"Fuck your garden, just because you've got one," George remarked with a cheeky grin on his face.

Sheila was the only one in the group who had some money, which she always said had been left to her many years ago by her rich uncle, who had died quite young. She lived in a large house with an acre of land surrounding the property near Cedar Valley. George, Terry and Paul all lived in small two up, two down style houses that just had small yards out the back, not far from Tommy's house in Travis Heights. A news alert rang from Terry's phone which he glanced at and put back in his pocket, not paying much attention to it, when a text came through on Paul's phone.

"What happened to talking these days? Everyone's on these devices," George muttered.

"Shut up, grandad, just because you can't read things that small," Terry chirped up.

"Cheeky little shit," George quickly replied.

Reading his text, Paul's face went white and still, like he had seen a ghost, and froze in a state that worried Sheila, who put her hand on his shoulder.

"Are you okay Paul?" she asked.

Paul didn't move or answer.

"Paul, are you okay?" She asked again, louder, in case the sound of the rain bouncing off the roof of the shelter had muffled what she had asked the first time, but again, no answer. Everyone was now looking at Paul and awaiting a reply when, without a word, Paul threw his cigarette to the floor and walked straight out of the shelter heading away from the side door that they had come out of. George was worried and ran after Paul, managing to catch him before he got to his car. Peter followed to see what was going to do.

"Hey, Paul, what's going on? What's the matter?"

Paul could not speak; he just pushed past him with an arm swinging out so he could get by and opened his car door. Looking back at George, and before he got into his car, Paul muttered, "Tell the dickhead I've got to go."

He got in his car, shutting the door before George could reply. Standing there, watching Paul drive away, getting soaked in the rain, George didn't know what was going on, but Peter, who was standing next to George, had a clue. He had read the text and knew that somehow Paul was involved, but with what? That was the puzzling bit. The message that Paul had got was very short and said, 'Be careful, another 1 sorted.' Peter stayed there watching Paul drive off, checking to see if there was any resemblance to the car that had driven away after he had been shot.

"I'm fucking soaked now," shouted George as he walked towards Sheila and Terry. And with that, the rain stopped. "Typical," he added.

By this time they had both finished their cigarettes, and were heading back towards the side door to The Factory as break time was nearly over and they didn't want to be late.

"Did he say anything?" asked Terry.

"Just to let the boss know he had to go."

"Worries me, that boy," remarked Sheila.

"Just get in, will you, I need to dry off," George said whilst holding the door open.

As the door closed, Peter was still standing, watching to see which way the car was going. He turned back and looked at The Factory where he had worked for many years, searching in his mind for a clue as to what had gone on. What was going on to cause Jonny to be a murderer, Tommy to have been shot dead, Paul to be so scared that he would run off so quickly, and now for his sister to turn up out of the blue? Knowing that he had to follow every little lead he could, Peter took one big thought and ended up in Paul's car.

After only driving for a few minutes, Paul pulled up at Billy's Burger Barn and sat waiting in his car. He was parked facing the windows that looked onto the highway so that Brenda could see him. Flashing his lights, he drew her attention and she waved to acknowledge that he was there, holding her finger up to say she would be there in one minute. Getting his packet of smokes out, he lit another cigarette and rolled his window down to let the smoke out and he turned the radio on. The news of a drive-by shooting was the first thing he heard. "Still no news about the drive-by shooting yesterday in Travis Heights, if you..." He quickly turned it off so that he didn't hear more, wound his window up and opened the car door. Waiting for Brenda just wasn't going to cut it; he had to see her now, and with urgency, so he got out of his car and ran across the car park and into the Barn.

Brenda was already in the back getting her coat when Paul burst through the door. He spun Brenda around and pinned her to the wall, grabbing hold of her throat with one hand and holding her mouth closed with the other so she couldn't scream. This was a different side to Paul than Peter and Brenda had ever seen. He was always the quiet one, not the one who threatens people. Or has this been his cover all along? Is he really a nasty piece of work, and one who has something to hide?

"What have you said?" asked Paul,

whispering in Brenda's ear so that none of the customers, Billy or the rest of the staff could hear what he was saying.

Brenda tried to shake her head in response but couldn't move and was in shock.

"Who knows about us? Who's been shot dead?" he carried on asking.

Brenda, looking directly into Paul's eyes, scared as to what he might do, tried to shake her head again but Paul had her pinned that hard against the wall she could hardly move at all. "Don't scream, because if you do, I'll make sure you never talk again," he said in a very threatening tone.

Paul lowered the hand that was on Brenda's mouth so she could speak, but still had her pinned up against the wall.

"I don't know anything," Brenda whispered, catching her breath.

When Brenda didn't answer what Paul was trying to find out his face changed again from anger to panic. He dropped the other arm that had been around Brenda's throat and started pacing the room, as he didn't know who it was that had been shot dead or who was after him.

"What's the matter? What's going on?" Brenda asked as she crouched down against the wall feeling scared and nervous from what had just happened.

"They're after me now," Paul replied.

"Who is?"

"I don't know. I got a text telling me to be careful, and then on the radio it said someone's been shot dead in Travis Heights."

"Who has?"

"I don't fucking know, that's why I'm asking you?"

"I honestly don't know what you're talking about as I've been here all day. Listen, why don't you stay for a while; Jonny is on his way round and he might know something."

Agreeing to stay with just a nod of his head, Brenda took him through to sit out front so that she could get back to work but also keep an eye on him, pouring him a whiskey to calm him down.

Knowing what Jonny had done the other night to that prostitute, Peter sat on the stool next to Paul, wanting not only to find out some answers, but to make sure he didn't do anything to Brenda.

"Just who are you?" Peter asked Paul, intrigued after the display he had just put on. "It's always the quiet ones to watch out for. I never knew you had that much anger in you."

As Paul sat there nursing his whiskey, watching the ice cubes melt slowly, Peter watched Brenda working. It was lunchtime and Billy's was getting very busy, yet every time Brenda came out of the kitchen with food, she would glance over at Paul to make sure he was still there and then peer out of the window to see if Jonny had shown up yet. The same pattern went on for almost 30 minutes until she glanced over at Paul and he wasn't sitting on his stool. She placed the two burgers she had in her hands down and went over to see where he could have gone. Looking around the barn she couldn't see him anywhere, so she walked towards the men's restroom and just as she reached the door, the front door opened.

"Hey, Brenda," Jonny shouted.

She quickly turned around and rushed towards him, throwing her arms around Jonny's neck.

"I think he's in the bathroom," she whispered into his ear.

Little did Paul know, but Brenda had been texting Jonny while he was on his way over to tell him what he had done to her. Jonny stormed towards the bathroom to check if he was in there.

"Stay out here, Brenda," Jonny requested.

She stood, arms folded, leaning against the wall, when Jonny came straight back out without Paul.

"Is there a back door?" Jonny asked. "He ain't in there," he added, searching the barn with his eyes.

She could see the rage building on Jonny's face and she knew that if he got hold of Paul now, he would knock him out.

"Yes it's over this way, follow me," Brenda replied, leading him past the kitchen.

When they reached the back door it was propped open by a fire extinguisher and a delivery truck was parked right in front of them.

"Where the fuck is he?" questioned Jonny.

They walked around to the other side of the truck but there was no sign of anyone.

"You go round the left, and I'll take the right," Jonny said as he pointed to different sides of the building.

Agreeing to split up and meet at the front of the Barn, they both walked around to spot any sign of Paul, and when they got to the front, they noticed his car was still parked there, but he had gone.

"Anything?" asked Jonny.

"Nope, didn't see anyone. Where could he have gone? Jonny, the text he received said people were after him and now we can't find him. What if they've taken him? What if they are waiting for us, what if..." replied Brenda, starting to panic and become hysterical.

"For fuck sake Brenda, will you shut up and stand still. I'm trying to think," said Jonny in a firm tone, cutting Brenda off.

Her hysterics and constant pacing around were starting to gain attention from the customers inside, who were staring at them through the window.

"Walk this way a minute as you've got an audience right now," Jonny said whilst grabbing hold of Brenda's arm, leading her away from the view of the windows.

He reached into his pocket for his phone and dialled Paul's number.

"Who are you calling now?" asked Brenda.

"Shut up a sec," replied Jonny very hastily.

A ringtone sounded in the distance, yet nobody was around, and as Jonny walked towards where the noise was coming from, he saw Paul's phone lying there in the grass, flashing Jonny's name. Picking the phone up,

Jonny looked back at Brenda who had stayed where she was, and showed her the phone whilst looking around again to see if he could spot anyone.

"They've taken him, that's his phone," Brenda shouted as she ran up to Jonny and grabbed the phone off him. She started to search his recent history as she knew his passcode from memory, just like she knew all her lovers' passcodes, and there had been a call from an unknown number just before Jonny had arrived.

"Well, anything?" asked Jonny.

Just as she was about to reply, a voice shouted, "See you next week!"

Brenda looked back towards the barn to see that it was the delivery driver, who was waving at her. She waved back and watched him get into his truck and pull away.

Still standing there waiting, Jonny grabbed the phone back off her and looked for himself.

"Oi!" she shouted.

"Well if you ain't gonna tell me, I'll look for myself."

"He was called right before you got here."

"Yeah, but no number."

"Must be from the ones that took him. Shit,

what's going to happen to him? What's going to happen to us?" Brenda's hysterics were starting up again and the only way to snap her out of it was to give her a slap across the face.

"Pull yourself together, and get back inside before people start asking questions," Jonny snapped.

With the look of shock on her face from being slapped, and holding her cheek, Brenda backed away from Jonny slowly.

"Don't you ever fucking touch me again. First Paul, now you, I've had enough. I don't know what the fuck is going on right now, and I don't want to if this is how people are gonna treat me. Pass me his phone back."

Looking down at Paul's phone, Brenda had pulled up his recent call list again and noticed that Paul had tried to call Tommy nine times whilst he was sat in the Barn earlier, and hadn't got through. She pulled her own phone out from her apron pocket and dialled Tommy's number.

"Who are you calling?" asked Jonny.

Brenda looked at him and held her finger up to silence him, but the phone just rang and rang.

"Have you heard from Tommy recently?"

she asked.

"Not since the other day," he replied, shaking his head.

Suddenly a female voice appeared on the other end of the line from Tommy's phone.

"Who the fuck is this?" Brenda asked in shock, wanting to know who this woman was, and when her reply came, she looked over at Jonny and mouthed to him that it was the police. His face changed and he shook his hands, gesturing to her that he wasn't here.

"What? No!" Brenda cried as tears started running down her face, dropping the phone down by her side.

"What's happened?" asked Jonny.

Not saying a word, she flung herself on Jonny, sobbing.

"Tommy's dead," she whimpered a few seconds later on Jonny's shoulder.

Jonny embraced Brenda, trying to calm her emotions by rubbing her back and stroking her hair.

"What did they say?"

"He was gunned down in the street outside his home."

Looking around nervously to see who was about, Jonny started to walk, with Brenda still in his arms, back towards the door they had come out of.

"Let's get back inside and get you a drink. I know I need one," Jonny said as he held the door open.

They headed in, making sure the door was closed behind them.

Earlier on, Peter had witnessed the phone call that Paul had received and had followed him to the back door when suddenly two men, unknown to Peter and Paul, grabbed him from either side and punched him in the stomach at the same time, winding him and making him crease over. The guy to his left, who was at least 6ft tall and built like a bodybuilder, grabbed both of Paul's arms behind his back and wrapped a cable tie around his wrists, when at the same time the other guy, who was slightly smaller and much fatter, put a piece of black masking tape over his mouth so he couldn't make a sound. The same man pulled out a black mask and placed it over Paul's face, completely blinding him. The two men dragged Paul's body to the back of the delivery truck that was parked there and lifted him inside, dragging him right to the back where there was an empty box. They threw Paul in the box, closed the door and placed a padlock over the lock. The two men exited the truck and walked around to the front of the Barn, watched Jonny walk in, and as soon as the door had closed behind him, they drove off. Paul was now trapped in the back of the delivery truck, the same truck which Brenda had waved at, which had pulled out of the car park, heading east on the 290 towards Austin.

In the far corner of The Wayward Inn, just on the outskirts of Sunset Valley, away from everyone else, sat April and Lisa. It was 7:30pm exactly and the bar was quite busy with people who had obviously just finished work. The chatter from each group was noisy, which is just what April had wanted, and was why she had picked The Wayward Inn in the first place. It had a reputation for being the go-to place after work, as that was when all the drinks deals were on. Whilst April sucked on her straw, almost finishing the first of her 'buy one, get one free' vodka and diet cokes she had in front of her, Lisa poured herself another glass of the house white wine which was only $10 a bottle.

They hadn't been there that long, but the drinks were going down quickly, April's because she loved her booze, but Lisa's because she was nervous when around her. Peter had also appeared, as he said he would, and sat down ready to listen into their conversation to find out just how they knew each other.

"To Pauline. What a wonderful woman," Lisa said, raising her glass to break the awkwardness in the air.

April lifted her glass and downed the last bit that was in there.

"Like I'd know. She never once tried to contact me after I left home."

"That's a shame," replied Lisa.

"Fucking blessing really, as she only ever fucking moaned at me."

"You should have been there at the end then, as she hadn't spoken for a while."

"I only wanted to say goodbye and good riddance really, which is why I found you when I did."

"Wow, caring sort then."

"Like you'd know."

Silence hit the table for a few moments while they both drank at the same time. April looked around to make sure no one was in ear shot, then turned back to Lisa.

"I saw you last night with Brenda when I drove past."

Hearing Brenda's name, Peter soon became much more interested in the conversation.

"And?" asked Lisa.

"You do know that's my brother's ex-wife, don't you?"

"No, I didn't. We've only been friends a few weeks and his name never got brought up," Lisa replied back. "Why?"

"Never you fucking mind, but this just got easier," April said with a grin on her face.

Lisa gulped down her second glass of wine and poured another before saying another word.

"Hang on. What got easier? What are up to, sis?" Peter asked.

April knew she could get Lisa to do anything she wanted right now, as what she had on her would destroy her. She downed her 2nd vodka and coke and slammed the glass down on the table, which frightened Lisa.

"Go and get some more drinks in," April demanded.

Lisa quickly grabbed her purse and

headed straight to the bar, which was very busy.

"I'm watching you," Peter said, peering in close to April.

Whilst Lisa was standing at the bar, still waiting to order another round of drinks, April was sat there, looking around to see who was in the bar and if she recognised anyone. She didn't see anyone she knew, but she did catch the eye of a well-built skinhead, who was standing at the bar only a few feet away from where Lisa was standing. She glanced down at the table, and when she looked back up, he was still looking at her. With a slight head gesture from this stranger, April stood up and made her way to the bathroom. She had only just managed to open the door when this guy flung her around and threw his lips onto hers, picking her up by the arse and lifting her up against the sink. With one hand he reached down between her legs and ripped off her thong with one straight pull, throwing it to the floor. As he reached back up to touch her breast, April with both hands was undoing his belt and jeans. She pulled out his dick and inserted it straight inside her. He was large down below and it made April scream with pleasure, so the guy put his hand over her mouth so they did not attract attention. He quickly flipped her over to fuck her from behind, pulling her hair back whilst she pushed up from the sink. As he pushed in really hard for the last time she knew it was over, and when he pulled out, she turned round and kissed him on the cheek.

"Thanks big boy, just what I needed," she said as she bent down, picking up her thong.

She threw it in the bin and walked out, leaving him still fastening his belt back up. She walked back over to the table where Lisa was now sat with the replenished drinks, winked and gestured to the toilets and waited. As Lisa's head turned she noticed a guy walking out, who looked straight over to the table the girls were on. She quickly turned back to April and they both chuckled.

"You didn't just?" asked Lisa.

"Too fucking right I did. I always get what I want, when I want it."

The guy didn't stay after seeing them laughing; he walked back to his drink he had left, took one last swig and headed out the main door.

"Another one I'll never see again," remarked April.

"You dirty slut," Peter added in.

April took a long sip of her drink and looked at Lisa. Putting the glass down, she slid it to one side so she could lean in close.

"I've got one last job for you and then it's all over."

"Anything," Lisa replied.

"Here we go," Peter said, leaning in now too.

"I want you to break into Peter's house when he's not there and find the deeds to his home. You'll find them easy as they are probably in a folder, labelled 'deeds', he's that fucking pathetic."

"Fuck you, you bitch!" Peter shouted across the table.

"Then meet me back in here with them. Once I've got what I want, I will pass you everything I have on you, and you are free to go."

"Ok, then that's it?" asked Lisa.

"Free," April replied.

Peter stood up, full well knowing now what she wanted: she wanted to take everything away from him, and now that he's dead, she could do so without a fight.

By the sound of her asking Lisa to go in when he wasn't there, Peter didn't know whether or not his sister knew he was dead, or if she was making sure Lisa didn't know anything. April was good at playing mind games, even as a kid, so Peter was still questioning whether or not his sister would have had him killed just to get the house. Passing over the keys to Peter's house across the table, April looked right into Lisa's eyes.

"You have 48 hours and I want them here. Fail me and I will hunt you down, releasing everything I've got about your dirty little secrets."

Looking very nervous, Lisa grabbed the keys off the table, stood up, put the keys in her purse, and walked away without saying another word.

"Wait a minute, they were the only full set of keys I had," Peter said. "Where the fuck did you get them from?" he asked April.

April finished her drink whilst watching Lisa walk away. She got out her phone and started typing a text. Peter got up and stood over her shoulder as he wanted to see what she was up to. The text read '48hrs, tick tock.'

Peter looked up at the door and saw Lisa

read her phone. She looked back over at April who just smiled and waved. 'Who was this evil sister?' Peter thought. 'She was never this bad as a child.' April finished her drink and left leaving Peter wondering what to do when he remembered Paul being taken in the back of the van. He had to go and see him, so with a thought, he turned up in the back of a dark delivery van, sat next to the box Paul was in. He sat there all night, wondering what was going to happen.

CHAPTER FOUR

Wednesday

The delivery van, which had Paul tied up in the back, had pulled over at the side of the road down a small alley between a row of trees in Barton Creek. They had been stationary over night so Peter knew they couldn't have travelled far. Although Paul had no idea how long he had been in the back for or whereabouts he was, he could tell it was morning as soon as the two men dragged him out of the back, throwing him to his knees; the chill in the air and the smell of the morning dew on the trees around him was a smell he recognised from growing up with his family in a log cabin high up in the hills.

The birds were chirping away and the

only other sound he could hear was an engine of a vehicle that was getting closer by the second. A large 4x4 with tinted windows appeared and pulled up behind the delivery truck, a car Peter recognised from outside Tommy's house. The driver's door opened and out stepped a stockily built, bald-headed man who had a scar running down his left cheek, dressed all in black with two guns placed on a back strap within easy reach. Peter could see that this was serious shit his friends were in, and somehow he was involved too. As soon as the man went to open the back door he knew this was someone's bodyguard. A gun suddenly appeared by the side of Paul's head, he could feel the cold tip touch his head and the nerves soon showed as urine appeared down the inside leg of his pants.

"Don't fucking move," said the man holding the gun.

Eager to find out who was in the back of this car, Peter focused all of his attention in the direction of the back seat.

A woman appeared wearing a black trouser suit, red high heels and large sunglasses that virtually covered the top half of her face. She was very slender, and looked like she was worth some money. As she started walking towards Paul, Peter tried to think where he had seen her before; he didn't know her personally, but had seen her face once before. Stepping up in Paul's face, the woman lifted the blindfold up just above his mouth and ripped off the black tape. Paul gasped for breath.

"How much do you know?" she asked.

"Nothing," Paul replied nervously.

Paul's reply didn't bode well as she reached her arm out and was passed one of the guns that the bodyguard had on him. She forced the tip of it right into Paul's eye and asked again.

"One more time. How much do you know?"

Peter, standing to the side of them both, looked at each of them, wondering what Paul was meant to know about, and who this woman was.

"Honestly I don't know anything, I don't know what you're talking about. Please don't hurt me, I've done nothing wrong," Paul pleaded.

She took the gun away from his eye and pointed it towards his shoulder, firing a shot which went right through, past his clavicle bone. Falling down to the ground, screaming in agony, his body hit the floor. The two men standing by him, the same two that had kidnapped him, picked him straight back up and put him back in the same position he was just in, with her gun back in his face.

"Please I beg you, it wasn't me, it was Jonny that made me do it," Paul said pleadingly.

Confused by all of this, Peter started pacing around shaking his head, thinking that one of his friends could have actually shot him over something he didn't know about.

"Thank you, that's all I needed to know," she said, lifting the gun away from Paul's face.

She handed the gun back to the bodyguard who had reopened the back door ready for her. As soon as she got in, the bodyguard closed the door, walked back towards Paul and shot him once, right in the middle of his forehead. As Paul's body fell to the ground for the second and final time, Peter couldn't believe it.

"What the fuck?!" Peter shouted out.

Another of his friends was now dead and he still didn't know why, and yet Jonny was mentioned. The bodyguard got back in the car and reversed the 4x4 to the main road where it disappeared out of sight. The two men who had driven the delivery truck picked up Paul's body and carried it further into the woods, throwing him into the dirt. They never once said a word to each other, it was like this was just in a day's work. They grabbed a few sticks and leaves that were lying around and covered up his murdered body, then returned to the van and drove off in the opposite direction from the 4x4.

The only things on Peter's mind right now were to find out why Paul had mentioned Jonny's name and what he was up to. These people weren't messing and more of his friends could die without him getting to know who had killed him and why. Then it clicked; the answer to where he had seen that woman before. It was at The Factory. He had been working the floor one day when he'd heard Tommy up to his usual flirting again, and as he had looked up to see which poor girl was being targeted that morning, it was the woman who had just driven away. But who she was and what she was doing in The Factory that day played on Peter's mind. Had she also killed Tommy like she had just murdered Paul, and was she now on her way to sort out Jonny, who was still with Brenda? What part does The Factory play in all of this, and why was she there that day? So many things were going through Peter's mind with so many unanswered questions.

Appearing back at The Factory, Peter wanted to find out how The Factory was involved in all of this, and if anyone knew the woman he had just seen.

"Any news from Paul yet?" Derek asked as he came up towards Sheila's workstation. "And where is Tommy? He's not been in for two days now and not even called," he added as Sheila looked up and shrugged her shoulders.

George popped his head out of his office and said, "You know what Tommy's like DD, he'll be trying to impress someone and will have whisked them away somewhere."

"Not good enough," Derek responded as he walked back to his office.

"Don't worry about him," George said as he came out of his office and walked over towards Sheila and Terry, who was sat only a few feet away from Sheila. "He must have woken on the wrong side of the bed this morning, he's been a dick since he came in, and it's only 10am."

Terry spun round on his chair and shuffled next to Sheila's desk as George walked over and leaned over her cubicle, "Do you think Paul's alright?" he asked them both. "He left really suddenly and I'm a little worried."

"He's dead," Peter replied to Terry's question.

"He'll be fine, I'm sure," replied Sheila, who carried on typing, brushing him off.

"Yeah, don't worry about Paul. It's probably family problems, they always come first," George added as he pushed Terry back to his own desk. "You just carry on with what you're doing and leave the worrying to me. I'll keep trying to call him throughout the day to make sure all is well," he said, patting him on both shoulders.

Walking back towards his office, George turned to Sheila and gave her a wink. She looked right back at him, her eyes glistened and she smiled back.

"I bloody knew it," Peter said, spotting George's face. "I knew something was going on between you two."

People in the office had taken bets when George started as they had found out he was single and wagered to see who would try it on. He was only in his late 40s when he had arrived and had been single for sometime before starting at The Factory. The first day he walked in, all the single ladies in the room, plus a couple of married ones, turned their heads to get a good look of the new guy. Peter had put money on Sheila being the one, yet George had never given anything away until now.

There was hardly any chatter going on on the floor, just the sound of keys on the keyboards being hit on a constant basis. You could see the occasional worker getting up to visit the drinks fountain near the elevator, but this floor was about work, work, work up until break time which was now only a few minutes away.

Sheila was very much into her keep fit and loved her yoga and as soon as break time hit she headed straight for the mats on the top floor, where she was followed by George, who liked a quick relaxation in the pods. Terry, on the other hand, was a video game enthusiast and always aimed to beat everyone's high scores every chance he had.

There were a few other workers dotted around on the top floor but many had gone down to the canteen for a coffee and natter in front of the television.

George had only been in the pod for 15 minutes when he came out and went back downstairs, texting whilst he left the room. Within seconds, Sheila had grabbed her belongings and had left the floor too, just leaving Terry and a few others enjoying their time off. Knowing that everyone was on a break, George and Sheila met up on the second floor where the huge hard drives were kept. The buzzing of the fans from the machines hid the sound of them kissing as she flung herself on him as soon as the door closed. This was something Peter didn't need to see and left them to it, knowing he wouldn't find any information out from seeing those two have sex.

Now with only ten minutes left of the break, Terry headed down to the smoking shelter outside and Peter followed. Terry, worried about Paul and Tommy, tried to reach them on their phones, leaving voicemails for them to call him back as there was still no answer. Terry was the youngest in the office and looked up to everyone who had been there for years. When Peter got fired, Terry had called him a few times to see how he was doing, but when Peter stopped answering, he stopped calling, thinking 'what's the point'. He then checked his news app on his phone as he remembered something popping up and had completely forgotten that night to check it out. Whilst reading it, George and Sheila had appeared, George wiping his cheek to get the last bit of lipstick off whilst Sheila fixed her hair.

"Guys, did you see this?" Terry asked, showing them the screen on his phone which had a picture of police tape with the headline 'Drive-by Shooting'.

George took the phone off Terry to get a closer look and read the first few lines.

"That's our neighbourhood," George remarked, passing the phone to Sheila to have a read.

"Bloody hell," she commented whilst still reading. "Have they released a name yet?" she asked Terry, who had read it all.

"It doesn't say," he replied, taking his phone back.

"It's Tommy, you idiots," Peter jumped in. "Paul's also fucking dead and so am I."

Looking at how clueless these guys looked, it couldn't be any of them, so Peter headed back to his house as time was running out for Lisa, who still hadn't been round and her 48 hours were nearly up.

Peter arrived back at the steps of his house to find the front door was already open. 'Was Lisa here already?' he wondered as he walked in slowly. He heard noises upstairs and headed straight towards them, which were coming from the bedroom. He pushed the door open to find Brenda going through the wardrobe.

"What the fuck are you looking for?" he asked as she was pulling things down from the top shelf.

Items of clothing were going everywhere as she frantically searched through every box and folder that was up there.

"Where have you hidden it Peter?" she questioned as she moved out of the bedroom and headed back downstairs.

Entering the living room, she started lifting paintings off the wall to see if there was anything hidden behind them. Now knowing what she was after, which was his safe, Peter knew she was after the money he had stored away for a rainy day. He had put bits away over the years ready for retirement so that the two of them could have gone on the trip they'd always wanted to, which was to see the world on a luxury cruise. When she chucked him out he took the money and it was just lying there, safe and sound, as there was nothing he needed at the time.

"Found it," he heard her say.

She placed a picture of them both from their wedding day down on the ground and started to wonder what the combination was.

"You should fucking know this, it's easy," Peter said, walking over towards her.

She tried Peter's birthday; no luck. Her birthday; still no luck. Whilst thinking of another number she glanced down at the painting.

"You soft bugger," she muttered as she entered their wedding date.

The safe opened and she saw piles of dollar bills stacked up. Reaching in taking them out, she heard the squeak of the front door opening.

"What the fuck are you doing here?" asked Brenda.

"What are you doing here?" asked Lisa, who had arrived to get the deeds to the house.

"Well I'm Peter's wife, so what are you doing in my house and with Peter's keys?" She had noticed them in Lisa's hand.

"April gave them to me as she needs something."

"What! Without asking Peter. You were just going to come in here and take it?"

"Looks like you're pretty much doing the same," she noted back, seeing Brenda helping herself to the safe.

"He owes me this and I need it."

"I need what I came for too, otherwise my life is ruined."

"What do you mean?" questioned Brenda.

"If I don't give April what she wants tomorrow she is going to release personal details about me that I don't want spreading."

"That evil little bitch!" Brenda dived in. "She's doing the same to me."

Peter, now looking at the pair of them, realised that April was blackmailing both of them.

"What is it she wants from you?" asked Brenda.

"The deeds to this house by 7pm tomorrow night."

"I need $10,000 before Saturday or this whole town finds out who I've been sleeping with."

"You don't need $10,000 to tell me, I know most of them already," remarked Peter, sitting down in the chair, looking at the panic on both of the girls' faces.

"The deeds are in the bedroom upstairs in a file labelled 'House Docs.' Don't ask, Peter's like that. Secretive in some ways, yet too fucking obvious in others."

"Fuck you," Peter remarked at Brenda's little dig.

"April said that," Lisa commented.

"And she can fucking talk," added Peter. "Blackmail, lies and deceit have been her whole life."

"Listen, take what you need to and get that bitch out of your life," Brenda said, pointing upstairs. "I'm going to do the same and we can make this look like a break-in."

"Good fucking luck," he said sarcastically.

Both Brenda and Lisa grabbed what they needed, and as they left, they pushed furniture around and tipped the contents of drawers all over the floor, making it look like someone had been searching for something important. Brenda wrapped her hand up and smashed the piece of glass near the door handle, leaving the door open slightly as the girls left and parted ways. Sitting back on his porch, he realised he had just been robbed by his own wife and couldn't believe it. The sun had started to set and he knew he would have to wait until the morning to get any more answers as to who had killed him.

CHAPTER FIVE

Thursday

After watching the sunset and sunrise on his porch, it was another glorious sunny morning, and time for Peter to get some answers. He appeared just in time at The Factory, as Terry had come across something. He got up from his station and walked towards George's office. Knocking on the door, Terry awaited a reply.

"Come in," shouted George.

"You got a second?" asked Terry.

"Go for it."

"I've just been going through some files to compile some new evidence with the bits of old things we have and noticed something weird."

"Go on," George said, leaning forward on his desk.

"Well it looks like some of the old files have been copied and forwarded to something. I've looked further and it's the old boss Peter's login information on the dates in question, and yet he wasn't here then," Terry answered whilst sitting down on the chair opposite George.

"So you're saying Peter may have stolen some classified information remotely."

"I've stolen nothing," Peter jumped in.

"Well that's the thing, boss, it says it was logged in from a computer on the second floor."

"Right, okay, I need a full list of everything he's copied."

"On it."

"George, you know me, I would never do something like this. Someone here has copied my login details and is stealing info," Peter said as George was exiting his office.

Walking over towards Sheila's desk, he leaned over her shoulders to whisper in her ear.

"Listen, we've got a problem. Terry's found a leak and it's from Peter's login details. I need you both on this; find everything you can."

George walked away in the direction of

Derek's office. He would have to inform the big boss as it would need red flagging and all systems checked.

"DD, we've a problem. Terry has found copied files with Peter's login details. Looks like they've been copied onto a drive."

"I want every bit of information as soon as you get it and I'll search Peter's files now. Who's on it with you?"

"I've got Sheila and Terry searching with me."

"Send everyone else home. This is priority. We've been compromised."

George exited the office and made an announcement to the whole office telling them all to stop what they were doing and to leave right away, looking back over at Sheila and Terry, gesturing for them to stay where they were. He waited until everyone was out of the door and went towards the pair, who were stood up near Sheila's desk.

"Right, it's only us that knows about this. We need everything on Peter," George said.

"What the fuck am I being blamed for here? I wasn't even here, even Terry said that before," Peter asked George as he was walking back towards his office.

They all sat there at their computers

searching away for an hour when Derek came out of his office.

"I've just been scrolling through CCTV and found something, everyone get in here now," he demanded.

George, Sheila and Terry all got up and headed to Derek's office to gather behind his computer screen.

"Watch this," he said and pressed the play button.

They all looked on and saw the back of a guy walk in, stand by a computer and plug in a disk drive. Only there a few seconds, the guy then exited but never showed his face.

"Do any of you recognise this guy?" asked Derek.

"Not a clue, DD," replied George.

"It's really difficult to tell, only seeing the back of him," remarked Sheila.

"No," added Terry, shaking his head.

"Well it's not me," Peter added.

"Well, he's our guy, whoever he is. I want employee records now of every male that works in this building," Derek demanded.

Everyone exited and returned to their desks to continue the search. Peter stayed to look at Derek's screen.

"Are you my killer?" he asked, looking at

the back of the guy's head.

"I don't care if it takes all night, I want this guy found!" shouted Derek from his desk.

"Fucking brilliant!" Sheila said, looking over at Terry.

"Tell me about it," he replied back.

Peter watched on as they pulled apart everything he had done over the many years he was there. This was going to take all night as there were years worth of paperwork, computer traces, photographs plus much more.

Looking up at the clock it was nearly 7pm, and time for Lisa to meet April. The only way of knowing what she was up to was by being there himself. The guys in The Factory were going to be at it for hours so no need to sit and watch nothing happen when he could find out some answers. With a thought he appeared at the Wayward Inn, April already inside, sitting at the same table they both sat at when they met a couple of days ago. It wasn't as busy as last time as it was Friday night and people didn't start going out until about 9pm in Sunset Valley, ready to party and bring in the weekend. There were the regular single old guys sat nursing their whiskeys at opposite sides of the bar just reading their newspapers and not talking to anyone, and a table of young guys who had started early, the ones who would end up just being thrown out early for being too rowdy.

The door opened and Lisa made her way inside, carrying a brown envelope. She walked up to the table April was sat at and slammed the envelope down in front of her.

"I'm done," she said with conviction.

April opened the envelope and took out its contents, reading them thoroughly to make sure everything was there, and gestured to Lisa to sit down.

"No, I'm good," she replied. "I just want all of this to end. Now hand over what you've got and I can go home."

"Now now, there's no rush," April responded whilst putting the paperwork back in the envelope and putting it in her bag beside her. "How old is your baby now?" she asked.

"So that's it, is it?" realising just what she was holding over her. "How did you find out?" she asked, slowly sitting down.

"Don't you worry about that, I have my ways. Bet your husband wouldn't like to find out would he?" April asked whilst picking up her drink and taking a sip.

"He was away a lot," Lisa started to try and explain.

"Yes but really, carrying another man's child and pretending it's his, that's some big lie to carry."

"You evil bitch," remarked Peter, not believing just how far his sister had gone to get what she wanted.

"How did you even know?" Lisa asked.

"I've been watching you for a while now. And not just you, by the way, there are others, too."

"I know about Brenda," Lisa quickly jumped in.

"That fucking whore has everything coming. I hate my brother, but she's a piece of work."

"Hate?" questioned Peter. "What the fuck have I done?"

"What's Peter done?" Lisa asked.

"That's none of your business. I am a woman of my word, so here you go." She reached into her bag and pulled out another envelope.

Lisa opened it and pulled out the contents to see what was inside.

"DNA is not hard to get inside a house," April said with a smirk on her face.

"What the fuck! You've been in my house?" Lisa said worriedly.

"Not me personally, but my guys say that your bedroom could do with a paint."

Lisa stood up and slapped April across the face with rage. "You bitch!"

Everyone in the bar turned to see what was going on, with the occasional cheer from the table of lads.

"Go on, girl!" one shouted over.

"Fuck off!" Lisa turned and shouted back at them.

Knocking back the remaining bit of her drink, April stood up and grabbed Lisa by the hand so that she couldn't walk away.

"I'd watch your back if I were you," she whispered into her ear.

Barging past her, April headed towards the door, walking past the table of guys when one of them stood up, blocking her path.

"Give us a kiss, gorgeous," he said whilst looking April up and down.

"In your fucking dreams, dickhead," she said as she grabbed him by the balls and moved him out of the way.

Reaching the door she turned back to look at Lisa, who was still standing there, now nervous as to what may happen and what had she meant by that.

"I'll be in touch," April said, and without waiting for a reply, left the bar.

Peter slumped down in the seat and looked at Lisa.

"You need to watch that one, she's worse than I thought."

"Shit," Lisa said as she composed herself and headed towards the door.

"Watch your back and be careful!" Peter shouted over, watching her leave.

Peter sat in the bar for a while, going over everything that had happened over the last couple of days. The only lead he had right now was the image on Derek's computer screen of a guy using his login details to steal information. Was he also his murderer? It was time to head back to The Factory to see what the guys had found, if anything. It was going to be a long night.

CHAPTER SIX

Friday

It was 7am and Peter was sat watching George, Terry, Sheila and Derek, who were still hard at work on the 1st floor of The Factory, searching through years of Peter's files, hours of CCTV and employee records to find out who the guy was on the footage, and how long it had been going on for. They had compiled everything that they could find together and had been sat around the same table that they had moved into the middle of the floor for the last two hours. Derek had written out an extensive timeline of events from when Peter had started up until last night to get a good overview of the situation.

"We need to go back at least 6 months and search all past employees too," said Derek, looking at George.

"Why, DD? If the video footage is from a week ago then they wouldn't have access to the building anymore."

"Good point, I'm tired and not thinking straight," he replied, rubbing his eyes. "Listen, let's all take a break and freshen up."

"Great idea," Sheila said, pushing her chair back and standing up.

Derek headed back to his office and shut the door behind him while Terry headed towards the stairs to go outside for a smoke, leaving George and Sheila alone.

"Postman's here," Terry shouted back as he'd spotted the van pull up whilst looking out of the window.

"I need a drink," George said as he walked towards the elevator.

Agreeing with him, Sheila walked past him and jumped in the elevator first. They headed up to the top floor to relax. While Terry was outside smoking, he waved the postman over.

"Listen, leave that with me and I'll take it in."

"Sign here for me," the postman said, handing Terry his device to scribble his signature on. "Cheers, have a nice day." He headed back towards his van.

"You too," Terry replied whilst looking down at what he'd just signed for. Reading it, he noticed it was for Sheila, so stubbed his cigarette out and took the parcel inside. Knowing that they were probably upstairs relaxing, Terry headed to the first floor and left the parcel on Sheila's desk, then headed back downstairs to the canteen for more coffee. Peter had stayed on the first floor looking over some of the files they had collected.

"Shit. Fuck me. There's so much been leaked. This is crazy," Peter said whilst looking at Derek's timeline.

Derek's door opened and Peter watched him leave the floor via the staircase, when suddenly a big explosion threw Peter out of the building. The fire alarm went off as Derek rushed towards the main door. Sheila and George, who were both in a relaxation pod, jumped out and, whilst running to the stairwell, noticed they were trapped on the top floor as the fire and smoke headed their way. The explosion had taken out the 1st floor completely, which had fallen into the ground floor, trapping Terry in the canteen.

The 2nd floor was on fire and sparks were flying everywhere from the hard drives catching fire. The alarm had already triggered an alert to the fire department which Derek knew would happen, so he waited outside for them to arrive.

"Here, follow me," George said as the smoke started to enter the top floor.

He grabbed Sheila by the hand and they headed straight back into a pod to shield them from breathing in any more smoke.

As the first fire engine was pulling up, Derek rushed towards it. "Hurry, please hurry," he shouted as the first guys started to get out. "There's three people inside but I don't know where they are."

Grabbing all of their gear, two firemen headed inside while the remaining guys grabbed the hose and started tackling the fire from outside. A second fire truck had just pulled up as the the firemen headed through the main entrance. They could see the extent of the damage all around as they could see right through to the 2nd floor from where they were standing in the foyer.

"Over here!" Terry shouted, trapped underneath loads of rubble.

They scrambled over to reach him and

started to get him out. Crying out in pain, they noticed his leg was trapped and seriously hurt. Throwing away the rest of the rubble around they pulled Terry out. He had a broken leg with multiple cuts and bruises and was lifted straight into the ambulance that had just arrived in the car park.

"There's still two more people trapped inside!" shouted Derek.

Running back in, the fire officers couldn't see anyone else downstairs and knew there was no one on the 1st floor that could have survived so they headed upstairs toward the second floor. Opening the door, they shouted in but got no reply, so left and headed to the top floor. There was smoke everywhere, making it hard to see anything, but George heard the shouting.

"We're in here!" he cried out, opening the door to the pod slightly, which let in tonnes of smoke.

"Are you okay?" a fireman shouted from the staircase.

"Yes," Sheila replied. "But please hurry."

The firemen made their way across the floor, guided by George's voice. They lead the pair back towards the staircase, rushed them quickly down the stairs and safely out of the building where they were met by Derek, who ran over and hugged them both.

"You're alive," he said to them both, grabbing onto them.

"Come with me and let's get you checked out," a paramedic said, pointing towards a second ambulance.

"Where's Terry?" asked George.

"He's on his way to hospital, he's got a broken leg but will be okay," Derek replied.

"Yeah, I'm fine," uttered Peter. "It's like I've been killed for a second time."

"What happened?" asked Sheila, pulling away from Derek.

"I don't know. I left the floor and then was flown down the stairs only just making it out. I'm so glad you guys are okay and not injured."

"We are too," she replied as she started walking towards the ambulance where George had already gone.

"Who did this?" asked Peter. "Someone really didn't want us to find out who had taken anything."

Peter stood there watching the fire being put out, not knowing if there was anything left whilst Derek, Sheila and George were taken to the hospital to get checked out.

There was nothing more he could do here right now until the fire was completely out, so he wanted to find Jonny to see what part he had in all of this. Knowing Brenda would be at work by now and Jonny had been all over her like a fly on shit, Peter appeared at Billy's Burger Barn sat right across from the shitbag himself.

After a worrying night, Brenda was back at work trying to act as normal as she could. Jonny had travelled in with her after spending the night at hers, keeping her company as he'd wanted to make sure she was safe. As he sat there watching her from across the room, he knew things were getting too much. Her hands were shaking every time she would hold the coffee pot and kept spilling it everywhere, apologising to everyone every time it happened. Jonny knew he had to rescue her as when she walked out holding a plate in each hand she reached the table and dropped them on the floor, smashing the plates and sending food flying everywhere. Breaking down into tears, Jonny rushed over and took Brenda into the back staff room, the same room Paul had taken her only a couple of days ago. She was a wreck and crying uncontrollably.

"Pull yourself together!" Jonny shouted, grabbing hold of both arms.

"I can't," she managed to utter mid-breaths. "What if they get us?" she asked, lifting her head to look Jonny directly in the face. "What if I'm next?"

"Why would you be next? You've done nothing wrong."

"But if I don't pay up, everyone will know."

"Know what?" he asked, wondering if they were still talking about the same situation.

"I'm such a bitch."

Jonny let go of her arms and sat next to her, putting his hand on her leg with a gentle tap.

"No you're not," he replied. "Maybe just a little," he added, trying to make her laugh.

"I am," she said and took a really deep breath. "It's my fault Peter lost his job, he was never meant to find out."

Peter, standing against the door just looked at Brenda. "Go on, tell him the rest."

"I'm such a whore."

"Bang on!" Peter jumped in.

"No you're not," added Jonny. "It was

only the odd time and we were just drunk and stupid."

"It wasn't just you Jonny, there were others too," she said, standing up and walking to the other side of the room.

"How many?" Jonny asked, now intrigued.

"Peter never knew about us."

"Well I do now," Peter added.

"He knew about Tommy because Tommy just couldn't keep his mouth shut, the stupid fucking idiot and now he's dead. He didn't know about Paul, and now he's missing. What if Peter did know and he's the one after them all?" she asked trying to put all the pieces together.

"Good luck with that one, I've been dead for days, like any of you fucking care," Peter said, walking around the room.

"Peter's not got it in him, he's too weak for that," Jonny remarked, looking round at Brenda.

"Fuck you!" Peter snapped at Jonny.

"Anyway, no one has seen him for months, so how could he know anything?" Jonny asked.

"His sister's in town and has been blackmailing me. I've got to give her $10,000 by tomorrow night or whatever she has will be released."

Standing up and walking towards her, Jonny was now slightly bemused. "She's asking for what?"

"$10,000 but I don't have enough. I went to Peter's house and stole everything he had in the safe but I'm a few thousand short."

"Okay, leave that with me."

"I'm not the only one too. She's been blackmailing one of the carers from where Peter's mum was and that's how she knows about everything"

"Fucking bitch!"

"Yep," added Peter.

"What if she already told Peter everything and that's why Tommy and Paul haven't been around?" she asked.

"She would want her money first before saying anything. She used to hold things over Peter many years ago, threatening to tell their mum about his past, so he paid her off. That stopped, though, when Pauline went into the home, as he knew it didn't matter what she told her as she would forget it anyway, and April left for years. Peter told me this many years ago."

"Well, she's back now," Peter said, "and

she wants more money."

"She's always been after money, the greedy bitch," Brenda said, sitting back down. "I need to see Peter and tell him everything before she does."

"Is that wise? You already think he may know already. What if you go missing too?"

"Shit, yeah. Can you go for me and see what he knows?"

"Yeah, no problem. It's been ages since I've seen him."

"Thank you, Jonny, that's why I've always liked you." She leaned over and put her head on his shoulder.

"Oh, fuck off Brenda. If you only knew what kind of man Jonny really is. He's a fucking murderer and you wouldn't want him anywhere near you," Peter added.

Jonny turned and kissed Brenda on the head. "Leave it with me."

Peter looked at Jonny who now had this look on his face that worried him. He knew he was up to no good and needed to watch what he was up to.

"Listen! You get back to work and I'll go and get the rest of the money you need," Jonny said standing up and walking to the door. "I'll pop by Peter's too and see what he knows. Listen, go home after work and I'll bring it round to yours tonight, if that's alright?" And with a nod from Brenda, he walked out.

"See you later," she said as the door closed.

"Don't trust him, Brenda, I know I don't anymore," Peter said, watching Jonny leave.

Brenda stood up and walked over to the mirror. Grabbing a tissue from the dispenser, she wiped the mascara that had run down her face from crying so much, reapplied her lipstick and tied her hair back. Brushing down her uniform, she stood up straight, took in a deep breath and looked at herself in the mirror. "I can do this," she said as she walked back into the diner to carry on with her shift. As soon as she reentered she saw the TV screen showing a fire on the news.

"Hey, Billy, turn this up will you?" she shouted across the counter whilst walking closer to get a good view of the screen. "Holy shit! Billy, it's The Factory, it's on fire." Quickly getting her phone out, Brenda started typing a text to Tommy, Paul, Sheila and George to find out if they were okay. Whilst waiting for a reply from any of them, she continued to watch and find out what happened. Her message tone went off and it was Sheila. Reading it carefully, she turned to Billy. "Everyone's okay but they are at the hospital getting checked up, thank god." She typed back and told Sheila that she would pop round tomorrow to see how she was. Looking back at the TV, shaking her head, she couldn't work out if this was an accident or not. "This is fucking crazy."

"Tell me about it," Peter added, and as he knew he could leave Brenda to continue work it was Jonny he needed to be with.

Knowing he had to find April, Jonny realised that without a car he didn't stand a chance. He walked out of town, followed by Peter who appeared next to him, for a couple of miles east on the 290 towards a gas station, which he knew had some cheap cars for sale not far from The Factory. He didn't need anything special, just a run-around, something to potentially burn if he needed to. It was only 10:30am but the sun was beaming down strongly and the walk was making him sweat. "Thank fuck," he muttered to himself as he could see the gas station in sight. Wiping the sweat from his forehead with his sleeve, he reached into his pocket to pull out whatever spare change he had, ready to get a bottle of water as soon as he arrived. He headed straight for the drinks machine which was at the far side of the entrance and waved at the cashier on his way past, counted out his quarters, bought a bottle of water and chugged the entire bottle within seconds, so fast that he didn't care about some missing his mouth and dripping off his chin onto his top. With a big wipe of his mouth he tossed the bottle into the bin and walked into the station. There was no one else around, just Jonny and the male cashier, who was just sat at the counter reading the newspaper, waiting for customers to come in.

"Hey man, how can I help you?" asked the cashier, looking up.

"I need a car."

"There's a few out back ready to drive away if you have the cash. Keys are on the front wheels if you wanna test."

"I'll have a look and be right back. Cheers."

Jonny exited and walked around to the back of the building. There was an old shed, obviously used for the minor repair that came along, and five cars parked up. As he walked over he noticed a couple of them were priced at $1000 which was too much to throw away for what he needed, then the fourth one along was only $600 and was the cheapest one. From the outside it looked fine, yet Jonny didn't give a shit really, as long as it ran okay. He grabbed the keys and got in, starting the engine up and giving it a few revs. "This'll do just nicely," he said, shutting the door and driving it round to the gas pump to fill her up.

"Found one you liked then?" the cashier asked Jonny as he came back in to pay.

"That should be right," Jonny replied as he handed over a couple of rolls of $20 bills and then shoved an extra $40 on the counter. "And that's for the gas."

"Have a nice day," the cashier said, but Jonny had already left.

He got back into his new car, rolled the window down, turned the radio on full blast and headed towards Downtown Austin. With breeze on his face, a cigarette in hand and singing out loud, he now had what he needed to get things sorted.

On arriving into Downtown, Jonny slowed down and turned the radio off so as not draw attention to himself. He didn't know where April was staying so he would need to keep an eye out for her, and knew if she would be anywhere it would be here. With all the drink and drugs she did it would be the spot. He weaved in and out of the streets of the town, passing all the shops, cafés and bars when he spotted her in a back alley with a guy. Pulling over, he watched to see what she was up to as he lit another cigarette.

"Who's that she's with?" Peter asked with an obvious silence afterwards. The silence was actually quite nice, Peter thought, as he'd just had to listen to Jonny sing at the top of his voice all the way there.

They both watched eagerly, intrigued as to who she was with and what she was up to, when they noticed her passing over an envelope.

"That'd best not be what I think it is," Peter said.

"What are you up to?" asked Jonny, leaning forward.

"It's the fucking deeds to my house, that's what she's up to," snapped Peter.

As they watched on, the guy rolled the envelope up and put it in the back of his pants and covered it with his shirt, slapped her face lightly twice as if he was patting a dog, and walked out of the alley. Jonny quickly slumped down in his seat so as not to be seen as Peter watched the man walk across the road and get into a car and drive off.

"Follow him, then!" Peter shouted at Jonny. "He's got my house."

Jonny, peeping over the dashboard, had another plan. He watched April walk down the street and started his car up. She flagged a taxi down that had just passed Jonny's car and he started to follow her. Keeping his distance, but still being able to see the taxi, Jonny followed April north on Interstate 35 out of town heading for Round Rock, and noticed it pulling up at a motel near Windemere, so he followed the taxi in and pulled into the car park, making sure she didn't see him. April got out of the taxi and headed up the stairwell to the second floor, going into a room. As soon as she was in, Jonny got out of his car and walked across the car park with his eyes fixated on the door she had just gone in.

"What are you up to?" Peter asked, following Jonny up the stairs. "You're not going to hurt my sister the same way you did that prostitute, I hope."

Jonny crept up to the window to peer inside and noticed April sat with her back towards them on the bed with her head in her hands. Looking around the room, he noticed her suitcase was open on the other bed and some of her clothes were hanging in the wardrobe.

"So this is where you've been hiding," Jonny remarked as he stood back to clock the room number. "Number 25," he muttered to himself.

Now knowing where she was staying, Jonny headed back down the stairs and over to his car, reaching into his pocket for his phone. He got into the car and started typing to Brenda. Peter looked over at the message, seeing that he wanted to know what time she was to meet April with the money, and that he had the rest ready for her. There was no need to hang around or wait for a reply, so Jonny started the car back up and headed back home to Blanco to collect the money Brenda needed.

Jonny arrived back home and pulled up his drive. He got out of the car and headed towards his front door, getting his key ready.

He opened the door and was met with a
punch in the face which knocked him to the
ground. Peter watched on as he had waited
in the car thinking Jonny would nip in, get
the money, and they would be off to see
Brenda. He saw two guys come out of the
house and grab hold of him, dragging him
back down the driveway towards a large
black van that had just pulled up. Peter was
up and out of the car and followed Jonny as
he was flung in the side door of this van,
followed by the two guys. As the van pulled
off, Jonny's hands were tied up behind his
back and a hood placed over his face so he
didn't know where he was going, which he
thought was pointless as the van didn't have
windows in the back anyway. As Peter
looked at the two men he didn't recognise
them at all. They didn't seem to drive for
long when the van pulled over and the side
door was opened. Jonny's body was flung
out on the street, sending him rolling in the
dirt. The front door of the van opened and
an older guy in his 50s got out, dressed in a
grey suit, open-collared white shirt, black
leather shoes and smoking a cigar. He
walked over to Jonny, who was still lying on
the floor.

"Jonny, Jonny, Jonny. You disappoint me. I was waiting for the next bit of information from The Factory and what do I see next? It's on fire and no Jonny in sight."

"The fire wasn't me," Jonny answered from underneath his mask.

"I don't fucking care! Where are my files?" the man said, grabbing Jonny's head.

"I'll get them, don't worry," he replied as his mask was ripped off his head. "I just need to see my guy on the inside and get them from him."

"What guy on the inside?" asked Peter.

"I've already warned you about what will happen if I don't get what I want," the man said, walking away.

"Don't you fucking lay a finger on her."

"On who?" Peter asked again as the man walked back over towards Jonny. "You best not be talking about Brenda."

With a heavy right hook the man knocked Jonny to the floor and walked back to the van. "You've got until lunchtime tomorrow or she dies."

Leaving him lying there on the roadside they sped off into the distance, leaving Peter looking over Jonny, wondering not only who Jonny was trying to protect, but who he'd had working for him in The Factory. Jonny found a rock close by and managed to untie his hands. Getting his phone out, he rang Brenda.

"Something's come up," he said. "Don't worry, I've got the money and I'll meet you tomorrow. Gotta run."

As he put his phone back in his pocket, Jonny looked around to see where he was. Knowing his neighbourhood well, he wasn't too far from home, and set off walking back with Peter walking with him. They got back and Peter watched Jonny head inside, pour himself a large whiskey and slump on the couch.

Jonny wasn't going anywhere tonight, so Peter headed to Henly, to his old house, where Brenda was just finishing cleaning the pots in the kitchen. She headed to bed, and Peter lay next to her watching her sleep. He had missed seeing her face lying there on the pillow, but this was now a completely different person next to him, as he thought about just how many men had been where he was right now. Not being able to get that thought out of his head, Peter went to the living room and stayed there overnight just in case anything happened.

CHAPTER SEVEN

Saturday

Sheila had just finished her breakfast and was putting her plate into the sink when the doorbell rang. Flicking the switch on the kettle as she passed, Sheila went to see who could be calling this early in the morning. She opened the door and was met with a huge hug from Brenda, who threw her arms around her, holding her tight. Peter had travelled along with Brenda to see if Sheila knew anything about the fire or about Jonny's inside man.

"I'm so glad you're okay," Brenda said, not letting go.

"Thank you, darling, I'm glad you came round," Sheila replied, patting Brenda on the back, hoping she would let go. "Come on in, I've just put the kettle on."

Brenda let go and followed Sheila inside. She always loved visiting Sheila's house as it was so much bigger and nicer than hers. With the money she had been left, Sheila was able to hire a cleaner who came three times a week, making the house look like a show home, nothing out of place, and the smell of fresh flowers in the air was something Brenda wished she had. Brenda followed Sheila into the kitchen whilst Peter had a look around. Sheila gestured with her hand and Brenda took a seat on one of the four stools by the breakfast bar which was adjacent to the centre island whilst Sheila headed to the cupboard above the kettle.

"Tea or coffee, darling?" Sheila asked whilst getting two cups out.

"Coffee please, white with one sugar."

"I didn't think you had sugar."

"I don't normally, but with everything going on I need it. Anyway, enough about me, what happened yesterday?"

"Well, I don't know really. I was up in the recreation room with George."

"Is he okay?" Brenda jumped in, interrupting her flow.

"Yes he's fine, we weren't injured thankfully. We were upstairs and suddenly we heard a big bang and the place filled up with smoke."

"You must have been terrified."

"It was very scary at the time but I had George with me, protecting me, bless him."

Sheila took a long sip of her black coffee and winked at Brenda.

"Still going then, I see," Brenda said, acknowledging her wink.

"How did you know and I didn't?" Peter questioned as he entered the kitchen, listening to their conversation.

"Been a while now. So come on, what's happening with you?" Sheila asked, pulling up another stool to sit next to her.

"It feels like I'm on a rollercoaster hun. Paul ran off on me on Tuesday. I can't get hold of him. Have you seen him?"

"What about me?" Peter added. "You never ask about me."

"I've not actually. Paul got a text at work on Tuesday, then just jumped in his car and left."

"Something is definitely going on as he was shit scared when I saw him. He was saying some crazy things."

"Like what?" Sheila asked, intrigued.

"Just something about someone being

after him and he was next."

"Next?" Sheila said, sitting back on her stool. "Next for what?"

"I don't know," Brenda replied, shaking her head.

"And who was after him?"

Brenda looked directly in her eyes and held out both hands and shrugged. As she did, she heard a creak from the floorboards above her, which distracted her and she looked up.

"Is he...?"

"Yes it's George, don't worry," Sheila quickly pointed out.

"Morning, George!" Brenda shouted.

"Stop it, you know he gets embarrassed," Sheila said as she clipped Brenda's shoulder.

Both of them supped the rest of their drinks as they heard George coming down the stairs. He came into the kitchen holding his mobile in his hand.

"Good morning, Brenda. How are you?" he asked.

"I'm okay," Brenda replied.

"She just came to check on us to make sure we were okay," Sheila jumped in. "Coffee dear?" she asked George, who just looked and nodded. "Another?" she added, looking over at Brenda.

"I'm okay thanks," Brenda replied.

"I've just had a message from Terry about yesterday," George said.

"Was Terry there too?" Brenda asked.

"Poor bugger, he was trapped downstairs and had to stay in hospital for more checks and get his leg put in a cast," Sheila replied. "What's he said?" she asked, turning back to George.

"He remembers going out for a smoke and collecting a parcel which had your name on it," he said as he looked up at Sheila. "Not long after he put it on your desk, the explosion happened."

"Does that mean it was aimed at you?" asked Brenda.

"It can't be. Who would want to kill me?" Sheila replied, pouring George's coffee.

"It could be someone that knows you," George added as he walked over to pick up his cup, "but listen, let's not think about that just yet, we're alive aren't we?" he said, rubbing her back.

"That's the main thing, yeah," Brenda added.

"No! I want to know who did it!" Peter said, sick of waiting for answers.

"Have you heard anything from Paul, by any chance?" Brenda asked George.

"No. Not since we last saw him at work at the beginning of the week," he replied. Looking back over to Sheila he added, "Oh and DD has asked us to nip to The Factory tomorrow to see if we can recover anything. He's going there today to make sure the building is still secure."

"Or cover his tracks," Peter added. Derek was now another name on Peter's list. Could Derek have been behind this all along, selling information using Peter's login details? He definitely had access to them.

"I'll get off and let you guys recover; you've been through a tough ordeal and if I hear from Paul I'll let you know," Brenda said, getting up from her stool.

"We will too," replied George.

"Good luck with that, he's dead," Peter piped up.

"Thank you so much for stopping by, it means a lot," Sheila said as she lead Brenda to the front door.

Brenda threw her arms around Sheila again, squeezing her tight. "Anything you need," she whispered in Sheila's ear.

"Thank you," Sheila replied, releasing her

arms.

She opened the door and Brenda walked out. As she got down the few steps she turned and waved back. George had appeared behind Sheila and waved.

"Look after yourself," he shouted down the driveway at Brenda, who had turned around heading to her car.

Peter looked at Sheila and George waving. "You two are no bloody use. I'll have to try DD instead."

Peter appeared at The Factory steps to find Derek sitting there with his head in his hands.

"Not found what you're looking for, or are you just upset that they are still alive?" Peter asked.

Pushing himself up using his hands on his thighs, Derek stood up and made his way through the front door. As he looked around the entrance the smoke damage was apparent. It was all over the walls like someone had taken black paint and thrown it everywhere, and the smell of burnt material was awful. He headed towards the staircase, touching as little as possible, as he wanted to get to his office to see what was left. As the door opened to the first floor there was a huge hole in the floor and ceiling and he could see right through to the canteen below and the server room above.

"Holy shit," Peter remarked. "Someone really didn't want anything found."

Peter followed Derek as he stepped over chairs, desks and computers to reach his office. The windows had been smashed through during the blast and the fire had clearly made its way inside, as the cabinets by the wall were black and all his pictures that were once hanging above them were on the floor, charred. Derek lifted his chair up off the floor and placed it back behind the desk, sitting down, looking around. He reached to turn his computer on, and to his surprise, it came on.

"Holy shit, it works," Derek said, pulling his chair in closer.

Peter walked around to see the screen to see what Derek was up to and watched the computer load up.

As they both looked at the screen they watched everything load back up fully, and nothing was lost. Derek got out his phone and sent a message to Sheila, George and

Terry saying, "All's not lost. We can still find out what Peter was up to."

"Cheeky bastard," Peter jumped in.

The phone then rang and it was George calling. Derek answered, "Change of plan, need you guys here now to get as much out as we can. See you when you get here." And he hung up before George could even get a word in.

Derek started to box up files that were inside drawers and unplug his computer when his phone rang again.

"Hey, Terry, how are you feeling?" he asked. "Great news, well make your way over here too, the guys are on their way."

Putting the phone in his pocket, he picked up a box and headed back downstairs, out of the front door towards his car. He opened the trunk and placed the box inside, moving everything he already had in to one side, making room for the computer. He closed the trunk and looked up towards the main road when he spotted a van parked up near the entrance. Not wanting to wait around, he hurried back in to wait for the others to arrive, locking the front door behind him.

Derek didn't have to wait long as Sheila and George were just pulling into the car park, followed by Terry, who had got a taxi in straight from the hospital. They exited their cars and started to walk to the entrance.

"How are you feeling?" Sheila asked, walking closer to Terry, who still looked in a bit of pain walking with crutches.

"Getting there," he replied. "They told me to take a few days off to recover but I couldn't leave this unfinished."

"I know what you mean." George said, reaching for the door.

He tried to open it but it was locked. George banged on it several times until he heard the lock open.

"It's only us, DD, is everything okay?" George said through the door.

"Come in, come in," Derek replied, ushering them all in.

Peter watched them all come in and, whilst looking outside, noticed another car pull up on the main road.

"Who's that now?" he asked, but before he could see any more, Derek had closed the door.

"Listen, guys," Derek said as he huddled everyone together. "We need to get everything we can out of here as quick as possible as I think someone is watching us."

"Holy shit," Terry said with a surprised look. "Who?"

"I don't know, but grab what you can that still works and load your cars up. We'll set up shop at my house for the time being until we can get everything moved to a more secure unit."

They all headed upstairs, being careful where they stood and went towards their own stations, picking up the little bits of information they could. George had grabbed his computer as that was still intact too, but all Sheila and Terry could get was paperwork that they had seen lying around on the floor, partly burned. Their computers had been smashed to pieces in the explosion. They headed back down to the car park and loaded everything into their cars, Terry putting his things in Derek's as he'd offered him a lift to his. Peter looked around and spotted the van was still parked up, as was the car, but in the distance were some more vehicles heading towards them.

"Get a move on guys, someone's coming!" Peter shouted as they continued to pack up.

They closed their trunks and all got in their cars, agreeing to meet up at Derek's house. Sheila and George didn't know exactly where Derek lived, so they waited for him to set off first and followed behind. They pulled out of the main gate and Peter watched them head towards the main road, knowing he would catch up with them later, when suddenly the vehicles he had seen came to a stop, blocking Derek from going any further. The van that had been parked up pulled up behind Sheila and George, blocking them all in with no escape. Men jumped out of the vans, all holding machine guns and ran towards both of the cars.

"Holy fuck! What's going on?" Peter shouted as he made his way closer to see who these people were.

Derek, Sheila, George and Terry were dragged out of their cars and were being held at gunpoint, while other men had opened the cars' trunks and doors, and were stealing everything they had just collected.

Watching on from the car at the roadside was Jonny, who had followed the guys there to see if anything was left. He had planned to get what he could to give to his buyers as his own time was running out.

"Fuck! Fuck! Fuck!" he shouted whilst banging the steering wheel and, as he didn't want to be seen, he quickly started his car up and sped off down the road. But it was too late; Peter had already clocked him and so had one of the guys from the van, who started shooting at the car as he left.

Terry heard the shots and went to struggle, which ended up with more shots being fired, this time directly into Terry's back, hurling him to the floor. As they tried to get Derek's computer out, he also didn't want anyone to have the information and grabbed it as it passed him. He realised he had made a mistake when he felt a gun appear on his stomach. Before he could say anything, and just looking at the guy in front of him, the gun went off and Derek fell onto his back, his head looking directly at Sheila and George, who were still stationary with guns aimed at them. They didn't want to die so didn't make a move, and watched on as all their equipment was loaded into the vans. Peter didn't know what to do. Does he follow the vans with all the information he needs, follow Jonny as he is now in trouble, or stay with Sheila and George to make sure they don't die too? Knowing it could be Brenda that Jonny was talking about when he was threatened, he had to follow him.

Peter appeared in Jonny's car, wanting to know where he was heading to. Jonny had been on the phone when he had arrived and he'd heard him saying, "Meet me outside Billy's now, I'll be there in 5 minutes." Jonny looked panicked and in a rush, definitely scared of something or someone, and was speeding down the main street with his foot flat down on the gas pedal.

They pulled up at the Burger Barn and Peter noticed Brenda waiting outside in her uniform. There were many cars parked up as it was nearly lunchtime and Peter knew that Jonny was going to be late, and now realised that it was Brenda that the man had been talking about. Jonny rushed out of the car and grabbed Brenda by the arm, pulling her towards the car.

"Come on, we've got to go," he said worriedly.

"Go where?" she asked, trying to pull away from him.

"They are coming for me, and now you."

"What?!" she screamed.

Jonny looked back at the windows of the Barn and noticed two men staring at them.

"Shit, they are already here."

"Who are?"

"Just fucking get in the car now! We have to move."

As they both got in the car, Jonny noticed the two men had already stood up and had made their way to the door. Starting the engine up, he put his foot right down and skidded the car out of the car park, looking in the rear view mirror noticing the two men rush to their car.

"We need to hide," Jonny said, looking over at Brenda, who was frightened as to what was happening.

They raced towards Downtown Austin, turning down as many side streets as possible so that whoever was following didn't notice them.

"What's going on?" Brenda asked.

"I'll tell you everything later but we need somewhere to hide and we need a new car."

Jonny pulled into a multi-storey car park, knowing that it would be busy as it was shopping day for many people. The choice of cars would be easy as long as they weren't followed. He found a space on the third level and reversed in so that they could see any cars passing by.

"Get down and I'll let you know when to move," Jonny said, ushering Brenda to crouch down low, leaving him and Peter to keep watch. They sat there for 30 minutes, watching cars go by and people returning with their shopping and loading their cars, then there it was: Jonny's escape.

April was passing by the car with a bag in each hand, heading towards her car that was parked 100 yards from them.

"Don't you dare," Peter said, looking directly at Jonny.

"Wait here," Jonny said to Brenda, "and don't move until I come back."

Jonny quietly opened his door and pushed it to, not making a sound. He crept behind the cars that were parked next to him so that April couldn't see or hear him. He waited until she had opened her trunk and was just putting her bags in when he rushed in and pushed her body into the trunk, closing it quickly so she couldn't exit. Leaving her in there, he rushed back to his car.

"Come on, let's go," he quickly said, opening and closing his door.

He walked ahead of Brenda, leading her towards April's car. She didn't recognise the car, but when she got closer, she heard banging from inside the trunk.

"What the fuck is that noise?" she asked.

"Doesn't matter, just get in quickly, we've got to go."

"Thank fuck for these touch start buttons, who needs keys?" he said, starting the car up and reversing out of the parking space as Peter appeared in the back seat, not wanting to miss anything.

"Where are we going?" Brenda questioned.

"I've got the perfect place that no one knows about."

They pulled out of the multi-storey car park and started to head out of town, driving at the speed limit so as not to attract any attention. The screams coming from the trunk started to worry Brenda as to what Jonny had done.

"Who is that Jonny? Tell me now!"

"It's my fucking sister," Peter said.

"I had to, Brenda, it was the only way out," Jonny replied, still looking ahead at the road. "It's April, and I know where she's been staying. You won't need to worry about that money anymore."

"Fucking hell," she replied, slumping back in her seat and looking ahead.

"What are you going to do with her?" Peter asked. "She doesn't deserve to die."

They headed towards Round Rock and when they reached the motel, Jonny parked up close to the stairwell to the top floor and looked to see if anyone had followed them. There was no one in sight so they got out and Jonny headed to the trunk. He opened it and quickly put his hand over April's face to stop her screaming. Pulling her out head first and holding onto her body so she couldn't hit out, he dragged her up the stairs as Brenda closed the trunk.

"Get her keys out, Brenda," he said, holding onto April as tight as he could.

She searched in all of her pockets and finally found them.

"It's this one," he said, reaching the door. "Open it up."

Brenda, frantically trying every key on the chain, managed to open the door and went in.

"Rip a strip of the sheet off, we need to gag her now," he ordered.

Brenda, now scared of what Jonny was capable of, ripped a piece of material off the bottom sheet of the bed closest to the door and passed it to him. He wrapped it around April's head and forced it in her mouth, tying it tight at the back of her head. He pushed her face down on the bed and reached into her open suitcase, managing to find a pair of tights that he tied around her hands, binding her from behind. He dragged her to the bathroom and, while passing, grabbed hold of the chord from her dressing gown, picked her up, and threw her in the bathtub, and then tied her feet together so she couldn't get out. He closed the door and looked at Brenda who was just standing there, in shock.

Peter couldn't believe what he was seeing; Brenda had helped Jonny lock up his sister, and was part of it now.

"She won't be moving for a while now, don't worry," Jonny said, walking past Brenda.

She sat down on the edge of the bed and put her hands through her hair, pulling every bit off her face. "What now?" she asked.

"We need to stay here for a while until I can figure out where we can go."

"So we're now on the run?"

"Until I can figure out what to do."

"This is ridiculous, what's going on?"

"Listen, I need you to stay here and don't

leave," he said, walking towards the door.

"Where are you going? What about her?" she asked, pointing to the bathroom.

"I'll be back soon and don't let her out, whatever you do. Also don't leave this room, as you don't know who's watching. I'm going to find Peter to see if he can help."

"I'm here, you fucking idiot, but if you are wanting my help then you definitely can't have killed me," Peter said, going to follow Jonny out of the door.

The door closed, leaving Brenda alone in the room with April tied and gagged in the bathroom, with nothing to do except wait for Jonny to return. Peter left with Jonny as he drove back to Driftwood, but when they arrived, Peter was nowhere to be seen. The house was still in the same mess that Brenda had left it in, so he waited in the car for a while. After a couple of hours, and no sign of anyone, Jonny had to get back to Brenda to protect her.

CHAPTER EIGHT

Sunday

It was 5am, and sat on a chair in the corner of the dimly-lit, dirty motel room, with the bedside lights flickering, Jonny watched over Brenda, who was laying down on one of the single beds in the twin room April had rented. The curtains were closed so that no one could see in and the television was off so the room was silent, and he had already checked on April when he got back, who was also asleep in the bathtub. He looked at Brenda, knowing that he would need to tell her at some point what had happened, yet didn't know how she would react. He bent down with his head in his hands when he heard Brenda roll over.

"Are you okay?" she asked, looking at him whilst lying on her side, head still on the pillow.

"Yeah, go back to sleep," he answered as he rubbed his face with both hands, looking very tired.

"I can't. I'm so worried about what's going on I just don't understand it."

"Brenda, you're not gonna like what I'm about to say, but I need you to listen to me."

"What?"

"No, listen to me," he replied as he sat on the bed next to her. "All this is my fault."

"What are you talking about, Jonny?"

"Have you heard from Peter in the past couple of days?"

"We've not spoken in weeks, you know that. I take it you didn't find him then?"

Standing up off the bed and walking to the other side of the room, Jonny held his head down.

"No I didn't, but I used him."

"Who?" she asked, sitting up on the bed, still very confused as to what he was trying to say.

"Peter. I used Peter."

"I don't understand."

"Not in the way you used me, just listen to him," Peter added, who appeared lying on the other single bed.

Jonny walked back over towards Brenda and sat on the bed that Peter was on, only a few feet away, facing her.

"I was asked to get information about The Factory and the only person I knew who had everything I needed was Peter. I asked Paul to hack into Peter's account and download some files for me after he had been fired."

"That's why Paul's missing? Because of you!" She sat up and slapped Jonny across the face.

"Listen! I had no choice. They were going to kill my parents if I didn't do what they said," he said, grabbing hold of her arm and pushing her back on the bed to restrain her from hitting him again.

"Who's 'they'?" she asked whilst trying to wriggle out of being held down.

Letting go, Jonny walked back and sat in the chair he was previously in near the desk at the end of Brenda's bed.

"I don't know who they are, honestly. I turned up at my mum's house one day to find both my mum and dad tied to chairs in the dining room. There were two guys holding guns to their heads and a woman sat in the chair at the end of the table. I had no idea who she was and when I went to go towards her a third guy came around the corner with a gun pointed right at me. I had nowhere to go."

"What did she want?" Brenda questioned, shuffling to end of the bed.

"She wanted information from The Factory by any means necessary, and if I didn't deliver what she wanted, they would be back to make sure I never saw my family again. I had no choice."

"Why you though? You didn't even work there anymore."

"I still don't know. Maybe because I was close to Peter, they knew it would be easy for me."

"You did what you did to save your family," she said whilst putting her hand on his leg to comfort him.

"That's not why this shit is happening though," he said as he brushed her hand off and stood up.

Brenda sat back on the end of the bed, now very confused, watching Jonny pace up and down.

"After the first lot of information I got for them was successful they wanted more, but so did someone else."

"Someone else?" she asked, looking even

more confused. "I need a drink for this," she said whilst heading towards the door.

"Where the fuck do you think you're going?" Jonny said, rushing to close the door that she had just opened.

"If you're gonna tell me some epic story about why I've been dragged into your mess, I need a fucking drink."

"You leave here without me, you're dead already."

She stopped what she was doing and looked right at him.

"They're not just after me, but anyone who was involved, and the man who was paying me more found out about me and you and threatened to kill you if I didn't get what he wanted," he added.

Not saying a word, Brenda walked right back to the bed and sat down. Jonny looked out of the door to see if anyone was there and closed it again, making sure it was locked.

"I never wanted this to happen, but I needed cash."

"Fucking cash! Fucking cash! All you had to do was ask!" she shouted back at him.

"These other guys offered a shit tonne if I handed them the info instead, which I did last week."

"So you're saying Tommy's death, and Paul's disappearance is on you? Where's Peter? Did he know what was going on?"

"Peter didn't know anything. That's why I wanted to see him last night to explain everything and help get you out of here. I don't know where he is."

"You fucking little shit! How could you do this to us? We've been mates for years and you turn on us for fucking money." Brenda walked towards the bathroom and Jonny followed. "And now this shit too, you have his sister gagged in the bathtub."

"I really didn't want any of this to happen," he said.

"Go fuck yourself!" came hurling back from Brenda.

He walked away, giving her some space, when there was a knock on the door. He looked back at Brenda who was still near the bathroom.

"Get in there and lock the door."

Walking towards the door, the nerves were showing as the sweat started to appear on his forehead. He pressed his eye on the peephole and there was Mr Walker, obviously wanting his information.

"Just a sec," he shouted as he backed away from the door.

"Shit," he whispered.

Returning back to the door, he reached for the handle and opened it to find Mr Walker holding at gun at waist height.

"Where's my fucking information?" Mr Walker said walking in, forcing Jonny backwards into the motel room.

"It was taken and I was scared," Jonny replied, now with his hands in the air.

"You promised and didn't deliver so you know what that means, don't you. My men are out now searching, and when they find her, they are going to kill her, and I'm going to make you watch before I kill you too," Walker said, forcing Jonny to sit on the chair and pointing the gun at his head.

"Good luck with that, mate, she's in the bathroom," Peter added.

A noise attracted the attention of Walker at the front door, and with a single gunshot to the head, Walker fell to the ground, followed by a scream from the bathroom.

"What the fuck?" Jonny said.

"Didn't you think we would find you?" asked Jessica.

Her bodyguard walked in and grabbed

Jonny, throwing him across the room against the bathroom door.

"Going into business with that prick, I'm not surprised you're now in this mess," she carried on, walking toward Jonny.

The bodyguard was strong and lifted Jonny's body off the ground and up onto the door, leaving his feet dangling. Jonny could feel his neck pulsating as he struggled to breathe.

"Trying to out-do me was the worst mistake you've ever made. Take a look at this," she said as she pulled up a picture on her phone of Jonny's parents, who had their throats slit open whilst tied back to the same chairs they had been in the time she had first visited.

"I told you what would happen. Paul gave you up and told me everything I needed to know."

"And then she shot him." Peter added.

The bodyguard dropped Jonny to the floor who slumped right down on the ground, gasping for air. Pulling out his gun, he pointed it at Jonny's head. Jonny backed up against the bathroom door.

"Please, no, I'm sorry," he begged.

"You double-crossed me and now you'll

pay," she said as she turned to walk away.

The bodyguard pulled the trigger and Jonny's head slumped over to one side with blood splattering the door.

A screech appeared again from within the bathroom.

"Who's in there?" Jessica asked, turning back around.

Kicking down the bathroom door, the bodyguard found Brenda hiding in the bathtub behind the shower curtain, standing over April, who was awake but still gagged so couldn't say a word. He dragged Brenda out of the tub and turned back around, firing another shot this time, killing April for just being there and seeing them. Brenda screamed whilst she was being dragged by the hair, into the bedroom.

"Shut up, Brenda!" Jessica shouted.

"How do you know my name?" Brenda asked, still with her head in the bodyguard's hand.

"I know everything." Jessica came closer to whisper in her ear. "You really are a dirty whore, just like they said."

As Jessica pulled away, Brenda spat in her face.

The next thing Brenda saw was darkness

as Jessica's bodyguard had smacked her over the head with the underside of his gun, knocking her unconscious. Lifting her over his shoulder, he followed Jessica down the steps of the motel and Peter followed too. He chucked her into the back of the car next to Jessica, who held a gun on her lap ready in case she woke up, and drove off. Peter kept looking out of the window to see where they were going, but also back at Brenda in case she woke up.

After driving for just over an hour, Brenda was woken up with a slap across the face from Jessica.

"Wake up, we're almost here," she said, sitting back waving the gun at Brenda so that she didn't do anything stupid.

They had arrived at the end of a long gravel driveway. It was covered by trees on either side and went on for ages. They pulled up in front of a large white house with four white pillars standing - looming - over the front door, looking very majestic. The fountain that stood on the roundabout in front of the house had a statue of a man on horseback rearing into the air with a sword high up in one hand, the other holding onto the reins with water coming out from all the way around the underneath of it. There was so much land with this property, and when looking around, Brenda couldn't see another house at all. She looked on, trying to find a landmark she recognised, but couldn't. Then, as the car stopped and the door opened, she heard the sound of drag boat racing taking place, and knew she had to be near Horseshoe Bay, as she had remembered that sound from being there many years ago with Peter, just after they got married.

"Follow me," called Jessica, as she walked up the steps towards the front door.

"Where am I?" asked Brenda as she was pushed from behind by Jessica's bodyguard.

"Fucking hell, this place is huge," Peter remarked, standing by the fountain.

Brenda looked around to see if it was worth making a run for it but there were men all around the land, patrolling like it was a prison. There was no reply from Jessica, who had kept walking into the house and, with a push again from the bodyguard, Brenda started walking up the stairs to reach the front door. The large double doors had been opened and the sight took Brenda's breath away. She had never seen anything so grand. There in the foyer of this large house, stood a grand piano enveloped by two staircases either side, which curved their way onto a balcony above, encasing a gigantic chandelier which seemed to hover in the big open space. Turning around in different directions, Brenda noticed doorways all over the place with men standing by them, arms folded like bouncers at bars.

"Who are you?" Brenda questioned Jessica, who had suddenly reappeared, holding a champagne glass full to the brim.

"A bitch, a murderer," Peter added, looking around the house. "A rich bitch and murderer, should I say."

Taking a large sip, Jessica did a full walk around Brenda, looking her up and down.

"Oh Brenda, Brenda, Brenda. What to do with you, hey?"

"I'm just a waitress, you can let me go," replied Brenda, nervous about the situation but also in awe of the wealth Jessica had.

"Were you and Jonny in on it together?

"In on what?" Brenda replied, trying to cover up what she already knew.

"Oh please, Jonny might have looked and acted strong sometimes but I bet he told you everything in bed."

"He was just looking after me."

"Whatever!" replied Jessica, who took another large sip of her champagne. "You wanted to know who I am," Jessica continued. "Well I'm the one that asked Jonny to get me some information from your husband's computer before he decided to double-cross me, and look what happened, his brains got splattered across a motel door."

Jessica walked over towards the piano and perched on the stool, crossed her legs and leaned forward, holding her glass with both hands. "How much do you know?" she asked Brenda, who hadn't moved off the same spot.

"He didn't say much, I promise," Brenda replied quickly. "All he said was someone offered him more money, and now my friends are gone because of him."

"Not just gone, Brenda, they're dead. Oh, and Peter's dead too, along with everyone else who had a part in this. You're the last one left," she said as she walked back into Brenda's face, tapping her finger on her glass, thinking of what to do with her.

"You killed Peter too? He did nothing

wrong," Brenda said with a look of shock on her face.

"I'd have kept him alive but someone else wanted him dead," she replied as she walked away, taking another swig of her champagne, finishing the glass. "If you want answers to why, you can ask them yourself. They've just pulled up," Jessica said as she walked away, under the stairs disappearing out of sight, leaving her bodyguard stood near Brenda.

"What do you mean, they?" Peter questioned.

Eager to know who had Peter killed, Brenda turned to look at the door. The sun was shining bright, which made it hard to make out who was coming up the stairs towards her.

"Brenda, darling, apologies for my sister. She can be rather ruthless at times…" Brenda suddenly recognised the voice and the look of inquisitiveness turned into a look of shock on her face "… but when your husband was fired, he ruined our operation and was of no use anymore. He had taught George everything he knew so had to go."

"How could you, Sheila? We invited you into our home," Brenda snapped.

"It was you?" Peter said, looking on in surprise. "How could you?"

"Oh, save it," jumped in Sheila. "You ruined it by not being able to keep your knickers on. It was your fault he got sacked in the first place. He'd still be alive if it wasn't for you. I hope it was worth it."

"You bitch!" Brenda shouted.

"Don't you fucking dare try and blame her," Peter said, getting up in Sheila's face. George walked in and headed towards Brenda.

"Where did you find this slag, then?" George asked as Jessica walked back into the foyer.

"Hiding with Jonny in some dirty motel near Round Rock."

"Is he...?" Sheila asked.

"Dead? Yes," Jessica jumped in. "And so is Walker."

"Good, good," George said.

"And so is Peter's sister. For some reason she was tied up in the bathroom, probably some kinky little thing they were up to," Jessica added, looking over at Brenda.

"You're all murderers, the lot of you!" Brenda shouted, looking at them all in turn.

"Is everything set up ready to go?" Sheila

asked Jessica as they both started to walk away.

"Downstairs ready and waiting," replied Jessica.

"Oh George dear, do me a favour."

Without any doubt of what she was asking, George pulled out the same gun he had killed Peter with and walked up to Brenda.

"George, what are doing?" Peter asked, looking at Brenda, who had started to cry.

"Would you look at that," George said, glancing at his watch. "Same time and same gun." George lifted the gun up and shot Brenda in the same way, right between the eyes. "Say hello to Peter for me."

"It was you! You bastard!" Peter said in shock as his body started to drift away.

"Bullseye," George said as her body dropped to the ground. "Now someone clean this shit up and get me a drink."

Finally knowing who his killer was, Peter could now be at peace.

Printed in Poland
by Amazon Fulfillment
Poland Sp. z o.o., Wrocław